Arthur I. Street

Handbook of the Venezuelan Question

And the Monroe Doctrine, containing a full history of the Monroe

Doctrine, President Cleveland's message, the Bear Raid on American

securities, and the complete correspondence between Secretary Olney

and Lord Salis

Arthur I. Street

Handbook of the Venezuelan Question
*And the Monroe Doctrine, containing a full history of the Monroe Doctrine,
President Cleveland's message, the Bear Raid on American securities, and the
complete correspondence between Secretary Olney and Lord Salis*

ISBN/EAN: 9783337399580

Printed in Europe, USA, Canada, Australia, Japan

Cover: Foto ©Andreas Hilbeck / pixelio.de

More available books at **www.hansebooks.com**

HAND BOOK

OF THE

VENEZUELAN QUESTION

AND THE

MONROE DOCTRINE

BY

ARTHUR I. STREET

AUTHOR OF " FINANCIAL CHRONICLE—PANIC OF 1893."

Containing a Full History of the Monroe Doctrine, President Cleveland's Message, the Bear Raid on American Securities, and the Complete Correspondence between Secretary Olney and Lord Salisbury.

DENVER :
THE TIMES PUBLISHING CO.
1895.

THE MONROE DOCTRINE.

Monroe's Message to the Congress of the United States, 1823.

In his message to the Congress of the United States in 1823, President Monroe used the following vigorous language with reference to the critical international situation described at length on the following page. Great Britain's ready acquiescence in the sentiment expressed contributed materially to the effect of the message and results were accomplished without any formal action on the part of Congress. This portion of the message has become known as the Monroe Doctrine.

"In the wars of the European powers, in matters relating to themselves, we have never taken any part, nor does it comport with our policy to do so. It is only when our rights are invaded or seriously menaced that we resent injuries or make preparations for our defence. With the movements in this hemisphere we are of necessity more immediately connected, and by causes which must be obvious to all enlightened and impartial observers. The political system of the allied powers is essentially different in this respect from that of America. This difference proceeds from that which exists in their respective governments. And to the defence of our own, which has been achieved by the loss of so much blood and treasure and matured by the wisdom of our most enlightened citizens, and under which we have enjoyed unexampled felicity, this whole nation is devoted. We owe it, therefore, to candor and to the amicable relations existing between the United States and those powers to declare that we should consider any attempt on their part to extend their system to any portion of this hemisphere as dangerous to our peace and safety. With the existing colonies of dependencies of any European power we have not interfered and shall not interfere. But with the governments who have declared their independence and maintained it, and whose independence we have, on great consideration and on just principles, acknowledged, we could not view any interposition for the purpose of oppressing them, or controlling in any other manner their destiny, by any European power, in any other light than as the manifestation of an unfriendly disposition toward the United States. . . . Our policy in regard to Europe, which was adopted at an early stage of the wars which have so long agitated that quarter of the globe, nevertheless remains the same, which is not to interfere in the internal concerns of any of its powers; to consider the government de facto as the legitimate government for us; to cultivate friendly relations with it, and to preserve those relations by a frank, firm, and manly policy, meeting in all instances the just claims of every power, submitting to injuries from none. But in regard to these continents, circumstances are eminently and conspicuously different. It is impossible that the allied powers should extend their political system to any portion of either continent without endangering our peace and happiness; nor can anyone believe that our Southern brethren, if left to themselves, would adopt it of their own accord. It is equally impossible, therefore, that we should behold such interposition in any form with indifference."

HISTORY OF THE MONROE DOCTRINE.

The Monroe doctrine is historically of British origin, and is an outgrowth of what seemed an exigency in European politics which touched British interests closely. That exigency grew out of an alliance for mutual protection against domestic revolutions between Prussia, Austria, France and Russia. These powers had met in congress in 1820 and again in 1822, and had agreed to support each other in suppressing armed revolts in each other's territory. Under this agreement a French force was sent into Spain to put down a revolution against Ferdinand VII. At first Great Britain consented to this agreement of the powers, although not a party to it, but after Lord George Canning succeeded Castlereagh as prime minister he saw reason to fear that British interests might be menaced by the alliance, and assumed an indifferent attitude toward it, which afterward developed into an unfriendly one.

About 1810 the American colonies of Spain began to revolt and declare themselves free and independent, and by the time of Canning's accession to power there were several Spanish-American republics whose independence had been formally recognized by the United States and practically by Great Britain. Great Britain had built up a considerable trade with these republics, a trade which was impossible while they were Spanish colonies, and therefore any indication of a purpose on the part of Spain to attempt to re-conquer these former colonies was regarded as a definite menace to British interests. In 1823 Canning thought he saw evidences that Spain intended to claim the support of the parties to the agreement of the year before in an attempt to restore its power in Central and South America on the ground that the revolts of these colonies had been a direct repudiation of the principle of the legitimacy and permanency of the reigning dynasties, which the allied powers had bound themselves to maintain by armed interference in behalf of the threatened monarch.

Canning called the attention of our minister to Great Britain, Richard Rush, to his suspicions, and asked if the United States could be induced to join in a protest against this apparent purpose of the allied powers, in an attempt to thwart it. Rush laid the situation, with Canning's suggestion, before John Quincy Adams, then secretary of state, and Adams referred the matter to the president and his cabinet, Adams himself being inclined to make light of the whole matter. Monroe and Calhoun and other members of the cabinet were, says Adams, "very much in fear that the holy alliance would restore all South America to Spain," and the outcome of that fear was the message setting forth the Monroe doctrine. The message was recognized in Europe as an important utterance and Spain tried to call a conference of the allied powers in 1824 to consider the regulation of Spanish-American interests, but the refusal of Great Britain to join caused the abandonment of the project. The message prevented the carrying out of any purpose of interference in Spain's behalf in America, and led to the early and formal recognition of the independence of all the Spanish-American republics by England.

The first appearance of the Monroe doctrine in our politics was almost immediately after its promulgation, its bearing on the part this country should take in the Panama congress of Central and South American states in 1826 being much discussed. The United States was invited to send delegates to this congress and did so, and the controversy over the wisdom of this action lasted for some years and was an unusually warm one, but resulted in practically nothing. Late when the Clayton-Bulwer treaty relating to the Nicaragua canal was negotiated in 1850, this doctrine was again to the fore and was exploited in congress and the newspapers, very much in the style with which recent utterances have made us familiar, but the well remembered instance of the French occupation of Mexico is the only case in which this doctrine has been officially and positively asserted by our government. Napoleon III. thought he saw in our distress in 1862 an opportunity to establish a monarchy in Mexico, and, with the sanction of the pope, and the approval of Austria he sent a military expedition to set up a limited hereditary monarchy with Maximilian of Austria as its first emperor. Our government protested several times, in spite of the indifference of Seward, but without apparent effect, but the end of the war, with the union restored and the whole country aroused, put a different face on the matter. When Sheridan was sent toward the Mexican border in March, 1867, there was nothing left for Louis Napoleon but to withdraw, which he did, leaving Maximilian to his fate.

Until the present exigency in Venezuela there has been no other contingency requiring any positive assertion of this doctrine.—Springfield Republican.

PRESIDENT
CLEVELAND'S MESSAGE.
1895.

On December 17th, 1895, President Grover Cleveland transmitted to the Congress of the United States the following message with reference to a boundary dispute of long standing between Great Britain and Venezuela. The United States had asked that England consent to a demand made by Venezuela that the matter be submitted to arbitration. After some years of negotiation, Lord Salisbury, at the head of the English government, finally refused to accede to the request. President Cleveland's message fully represents the position of the United States. Its emphatic and extraordinary nature created marked excitement throughout the United States and Europe.

To Congress—In my annual message addressed to the Congress on the third instant, I called attention to the pending boundary controversy between Great Britain and the republic of Venezuela, and recited the substance of a representation made by this government, to her Britannic majesty's government, suggesting reasons why such disputes should be submitted to arbitration for settlement, and inquiring whether it would be so submitted.

The answer of the British government, which was then awaited, has since been received, and together with the dispatch to which it is a reply is hereto appended. Such reply is embodied in two communications addressed by the British prime minister to Sir Julian Pauncefote, the British ambassador at this capital. It will be seen that one of these communications is devoted exclusively to observations upon the Monroe doctrine, and claims that in the present instance a new and strange extension and development of this doctrine is insisted on by the United States; that the reasons justifying an appeal to the doctrine enunciated by President Monroe are generally inapplicable "to the state of things in which we live at the present day," and especially inapplicable to a controversy involving the boundary line between Great Britain and Venezuela.

Without attempting extended arguments in reply to these positions it may not be amiss to suggest that the doctrine upon which we stand is strong and sound, because its enforcement is important to our peace and safety as a nation and is essential to the integrity of our free institutions and the tranquil maintenance of our distinctive form of government. It was intended to apply to every stage of our national life, and cannot become obsolete while our republic endures. If the balance of power is justly a cause for jealous anxiety among the governments of the old world, and a subject for our absolute non-interference, none the less is an observance of the Monroe doctrine of vital concern to our people and their government.

—Assuming, therefore, that we may properly insist upon the doctrine without regard to "the state of things in which we live," or any changed conditions here or elsewhere, it is not apparent why its application may not be invoked in the present controversy. If a European power, by an extension of its boundaries, takes possession of the territory of one of our neighboring republics against its will and in derogation of its rights, it is difficult to see why, to that extent, such European power does not thereby attempt to extend its system of government to that portion of this continent which is thus taken. This is the precise action which President Monroe declared to be "dangerous to our peace and safety," and it can make no difference whether the European system is extended by an advance of frontier or otherwise.

It is also suggested in the British reply that we should not seek to apply the Monroe doctrine to the pending dispute, because it does not embody any principle of international law which "is founded on the general consent of nations," and "that no statesman, however eminent, and no nation, however powerful, are competent to insert into the code of international law a novel principle which was never recognized before and which has not since been accepted by the governments of any other country."

Practically the principle for which we contend has peculiar, if not exclusive relation to the United States. It may not have been admitted in so many words to the code of international law, but since in international councils every nation is entitled to the rights belonging to it, if the enforcement of the Monroe doctrine is something we may justly claim, it has its place in the code of international law as certainly and as securely as if it were specifically mentioned, and when . the United States is a suitor before the high tribunal that administers international law, the question to be determined is whether or not we present claims which the justice of that code of law find to be right and valid.

The Monroe doctrine finds its recognition in those principles of international law which are based upon the theory that every nation shall have its rights protected and its just claims enforced.

Of course, this government is entirely confident that under the sanction of this doctrine we have clear rights and undoubted claims. Nor is this ignored in the British reply. The prime minister, while not admitting that the Monroe doctrine is applicable to present conditions, states: "In declaring that the United States would resist any such enterprise if it was contemplated," President Monroe adopted a policy which received the entire sympathy of the English government of that date. He further declares: "Though the language of President Mon-

roe is directed to the attainment of objects which most Englishmen would agree to be salutary, it is impossible to admit that they have been inscribed by any adequate authority in the code of international law."

Again he says: "They (her majesty's government) fully concur with the view which President Monroe apparently entertained, that any disturbance of the existing territorial distribution in that hemisphere by any fresh acquisitions on the part of any European state would be a highly inexpedient change."

In the belief that the doctrine for which we contend was clear and definite, that it was founded upon substantial considerations and involved our safety and welfare, that it was fully applicable to our present conditions and to the state of the world's progress, and that it was directly related to the pending controversy and without any conviction as to the final merits of the dispute, but anxious to learn in a satisfactory and conclusive manner whether Great Britain sought, under a claim of boundary, to extend her possessions on this continent without right, or whether she merely sought possession of territory facility included within her lines of ownership, this government proposed to the government of Great Britain a resort to arbitration as the proper means of settling the question to the end that a vexatious boundary dispute between two contestants might be determined and our exact standing and relation in respect to the controversy might be made clear.

It will be seen from the correspondence herewith submitted that this proposition has been declined by the British government upon the grounds which, under the circumstances seem to me to be far from satisfactory. It is deeply disappointing that such an appeal, actuated by the most friendly feelings towards both nations directly concerned, addressed to the sense of justice and to the magnanimity of one of the great powers of the world and touching its relations to one comparatively weak and small, should have produced no better results.

The course to be pursued by this government in view of the present condition does not appear to admit of serious doubt. Having labored faithfully for many years to induce Great Britain to submit this dispute to impartial arbitration, and having been now finally apprised of her refusal to do so, nothing remains but to accept the situation, to recognize its plain requirements and deal with it accordingly. Great Britain's present proposition has never thus far been regarded as admissible by Venezuela, though any adjustment of the boundary which that country may deem for her advantage and may enter into of her own free will cannot, of course, be objected to by the United States. Assuming, however, that the attitude of Venezuela will remain unchanged, the dispute has reached such a stage as to make it now incumbent upon the United States to take measures to determine with sufficient certainty for its justification what is the true divisional line between the republic of Venezuela and British Guiana. The inquiry to that end should, of course, be conducted carefully and judicially and due weight should be given to all available evidence, records and facts in support of the claims of both parties.

In order that such an examination should be prosecuted in a thorough and satisfactory manner, I suggest that the congress make an adequate appropriation for the expenses of a commission to be appointed by the executive, who shall make the necessary investigation and report upon the matter with the least possible delay. When such report is made and accepted it will, in my opinion, be the duty of the United States to resist by every means in its power as a willful aggression upon its rights and interests, the appropriation by Great Britain of any lands or the exercise of governmental jurisdiction over any territory which, after investigation, we have determined of right belongs to Venezuela.

In making these recommendations I am fully alive to the responsibility incurred and keenly realize al the consequences that may follow.

I am, nevertheless, firm in my conviction that while it is a grievous thing to contemplate the two great English speaking peoples of the world as being otherwise than friendly competitors in the onward march of civilization and strenuous and worthy rivals in all the arts of peace, there is no calamity which a great nation can invite which equals that which follows a supine submission to wrong and injustice and the consequent loss of national self-respect and honor, beneath which is shielded and defended a people's safety and greatness.

(Signed)   GROVER CLEVELAND.
Executive Mansion, Dec. 17, 1895.

AMERICANS AROUSED.

Eight Days of Excitement Throughout the United States.

TUESDAY, DECEMBER 17, 1895.

President Cleveland transmits his Venezuelan message to congress. It is received with applause in both Senate and House without regard to party lines. The American press, with the exception of the *New York World* and *Post* and the *Baltimore Sun*, approve it. The English press is almost unanimous in resentment, attributing the mesage to political motives.

The Executive committee of the council of the Irish National Alliance of America passes resolutions offering 100,000 Irish soldiers in event of war with England arising from the President's message.

The Confederate Veterans Camp, of New York, offers a company of Confederate veterans in case of war.

Bears on the New York Stock Exchange begin an attack on all classes of stocks.

WEDNESDAY, DECEMBER 18th, 1895.

The House of Representatives passes a bill giving the President authority to appoint a commission to investigate the Venezuelan boundary according to the recommendations of his message, and appropriating $100,000 for the expenses of the commission.

Bills are offered in both houses of Congress appropriating $100,000,000, to be raised by popular loan, to strengthen the national defenses.

Messages received at the White House from all portions of the country and from all political parties congratulating the President on his message.

The hostile tone of the British press seems to arouse the war spirit throughout the United States.

Lord Salisbury manifests anxiety when the text of the President's message is transmitted to him.

Many continential papers of Europe take a stand against the Monroe Doctrine.

Ambassador Bayard delivers a speech at a dinner in London of the Actors Fund Benefit in which he speaks of the American and English peoples as "children of brain and heart, born of common ancestry, who could not be divided."

The President's message is read before Company C,, of the Indiana National Guard, at Anderson, Indiana., and before the entire high school at Buffalo, New York.

Directors of the American Humane Education Society and Massachusetts Society for Prevention of Cruelty to Animals pass resolutions calling on the "God of Battles" to prevent war.

The Virginia House of Delegates unanimously adopts a resolution upholding the President.

An Alabama citizen offers to raise and equip a regiment for war.

Judge Grosscup, at Peoria, Ills., praises the message from the bench.

Union veterans of New York endorse the President and offer support if it be needed.

The First Infantry, National Guard of Missouri, writes the President that it is ready or service.

The Freeman's Journal of Ireland thinks Lord Salisbury will have to recede from his position.

Canadian papers say, "They may make us suffer but they cannot make us yield."

Governor Altgeld, of Illinois, criticises the message disapprovingly.

Venezuela generally rejoices. Caracas is *en fete.* The women boycott English manufacturers.

The Manchester (England) Stock Exchange goes into a panic. Operators on all European bourses are alarmed. The opinion is expressed that the message will render the placing of more United States bonds in London impossible.

A theatrical audience in Denver applauds an anti-English sentiment in the play of Marmion, where England is spoken of as "the most traitorous and treacherous of nations."

As the day progresses a general scare develops in financial circles. London begins nloading American securities, selling 25,000 to 30,000 shares in the morning market.

American bears on the New York Exchange take advantage of the situation and crowd Industrials" for sale. Sugar refining, in which few or no shares are held abroad, closes one per cent. off. The market closes with all stocks lower. The foreign selling of the morning was in Louisville and Nashville, St. Paul, Southern Railway, and M. K. & T. selling influences exchange and rates for sterling advance to $4.88½ and $4.90, presaging old exports.

THURSDAY, DECEMBER 19, 1895.

The Senate unanimously agrees to commit the House bill on the Venezuela Commission to the Committee on Foreign Relations, discussing the message with dignity and deliberation and without exception endorsing the President's definition of the Monroe Doctrine. "It is too big a question for party purposes and party gain," says Senator Teller. Our politics stop at the water's edge," says Senator Lodge.

The British press thinks it discovers in the deliberation of the Senate a change in the tone of the American public. However, the *Westminster Gazette* expresses the opinion that Lord Salisbury played into President Cleveland's hands by attacking the Monroe Doctrine unnecessarily. Many papers like the *Pall Mall Gazette* treat the whole matter as a joke and "wonder when will come the relieving laugh, for with that Anglo-Saxon peal we shall, for the first time, hear the true voice of America."

At the annual dinner of the British Public Schools and Universities Association in New York, Rev. Jocelyn Johnstone says, "The man who threatens war is a traitor to humanity itself."

The Berlin *Kreuz Zeitung* says, "England must remember that the time has gone by when the growl of the lion sufficed to secure advantages where it had no rights." The *ossische Zeitung* counsels European support of England "lest Yankeedom should come to believe it has but to command the old continent to obey."

The Virginia Senate upholds the President by divided vote.

The Hibernian Rifles of Wilkesbarre, Pa., tender their services to the President in the event of war.

Hale, of Maine, introduces a bill into the Senate for the construction of six battle ships and twenty-five torpedo boats.

Leading bankers and brokers in London hold a meeting to consider the financial aspect of the Venezuelan matter, and to discuss international credits. They decide to postpone action to ascertain the later and "cooler" American sentiment. Nevertheless the market opens with heavy sales, and closes with more offerings than buyers, and with money more favorable to lenders than borrowers. International stocks suffer heavily, St. Paul

showing the greatest decline, its stock being held largely abroad. Heavy declines are
noted in comparatively inactive stocks, such as Consolidated Gas, Jersey Central and
others, indicating that a large percentage of the sales arise from the short interests. An
nouncement that gold shipments on Saturday will aggregate $4,000,000 causes a flurry in
call loans. It begins to be apparent that capital generally is anxious over the situation.

FRIDAY, DECEMBER 20, 1895.

The day opens with Wall street in a scare, and London hammering American securities
The Senate passes the House bill for the Venezuelan commission, voting down all
amendments Senator Lodge declares that London's calling in of loans is not honorable
and will not frighten the American people.

American securities jump two and four points between sales in London. Threats are
circulated of return of securities from everywhere, frightening New York and starting the
calling of money loans. A consequent shifting of obligations is reflected in the rise of
money rates which jump up to 6, 12, 15, 25 and 50 per cent in rapid succession, some loan
being made at 80 per cent. Three small firms on Wall Street fail. The feeling of anxiety
becomes intensified. Rumors are circulated that the clearing house has called a meeting
to consider issuing loan certificates. The only reassuring sign is that there is no special
demand for money, the apprehension seeming to come from small lenders. The decline in
stock becomes serious. St. Paul falls off ten points; Sugar Refining, Chicago Gas, Rock
Island, Louisville & Nashville, Missouri Pacific, Southern Ry. preferred, and U. S. Leather
fluctuates violently from five to eight points down. At times stocks can hardly be sold.

Senator Sherman's speech on the Venezuelan Commission bill, counseling deliberation, and the unexpected announcement that only $3,100,000 of gold is to be shipped on
Saturday strengthens the market in the afternoon, but the strain on the street has been
so great that five more firms fail. Sentiment in some quarters begins to turn against the
President. Stocks seem to be forced up and down for effect.

President Cleveland transmits to Congress the following message urging financial legislation. It is preceded by an excited Cabinet meeting which adjourns long enough to
allow the President to write the message.

FINANCIAL MESSAGE.

To the Congress:—In my last message, the evils of our present financial system were
plainly pointed out, and the causes and means of the depletion of government gold were
explained. It was therein stated that after all the efforts that had been made by the executive branch of the government to protect our gold reserve by the issuance of bonds
amounting to more than $162,000,000, such reserve then amounted to but little more than
$79,000,000 that about $16,000,000 had been withdrawn from such reserve, during the month
next previous to the date of that message and quite large withdrawals for shipment in
the immediate future were predicted.

The contingency then feared has reached us, and the withdrawal of gold since the
communication referred to and others that appear inevitable, threatening such a depletion in our government gold reserve as brings us face to face with the necessity of further
action for its protection. This condition is intensified by the prevalence in certain
quarters of sudden and unusual apprehension and timidity in business circles.

We are in the midst of another season of perplexity, caused by our dangerous and
fatuous financial operations. These may be expected to recur with certainty as long as
there is no amendment in our financial system. If in this particular instance our predicament is at all influenced by a recent insistence upon the position we should occupy in
our relation to certain questions concerning our foreign policy, this furnishes a signal and
impressive warning that even the patriotic sentiment of our people is not an adequate
substitute for a sound financial policy.

Of course there can be no doubt in any thoughtful mind as to the complete solvency of our nation, nor can there be any just apprehension that the American people will be satisfied with less than an honest payment of our public obligations in the recognized money of the world. We should not overlook the fact, however, that aroused fear is unreasoning and must be taken into account in all efforts to avert public loss end sacrifice of our people's interests.

The real and sensible cure for our recurring troubles can only be effected by a complete change in our financial scheme. Pending that the executive branch of the government will not relax its efforts nor abandon its determination to use every means within its reach to maintain before the world American credit, nor will there be any hesitation in exhibiting its confidence in the resources of our country and the constant patriotism of our people.

In view, however, of the peculiar situation now confronting us, I have ventured to herein express the earnest hope that the Congress, in default of inauguration of a better system of finance, will not take a recess from its labors before it has, by legislative enactment or declaration, done something, not only to remind those apprehensive among our people that the resources of this government and a scrupulous regard for honest dealing, affords sure guarantee of unquestioned safety and soundness, but to reassure the world that, with these factors and the patriotism of our citizens, the ability and determination of our nation to meet in any circumstances every obligation it incurs, do not admit of question.

I ask, at the hands of the Congress, such prompt aid as it alone has the power to give, to prevent, in a time of fear and apprehension, any sacrifice of the peoples' interests and the public funds or the impairment of our public credit in an effort by the executive action to relieve the dangers of the present contingency.

GROVER CLEVELAND,

Executive Mansion, December 20, 1895.

After the above message was read the Senate adjourned till Saturday.

The *Novoe Vremja*, of St. Petersburg, Russia, predicts, in event of war between the United States and England "an hour of bitter retribution for a past upon which Englishmen pride themselves, forgetting that successes gained by guile and force are never enduring."

A meeting of influential citizens in Panama calls a demonstration for the 23d "intended to be demonstrative of the gratitude of South America" for President Cleveland's message.

Wheat and cotton break 1⅝ cents and 15 points respectively; then comes heavy buying which England takes a hand.

Denver mining stocks drops five to fifteen points. Chicago and Philadelphia stock exchanges respond to the general slump. Also Montreal Exchange.

Some Boston bankers petition for a meeting of the exchange to appoint a commission to go to Washington in protest against the political situation.

President Austin Scott of Rutgers College calls President Cleveland the "king of Jingoes," and says the country is "drunk with passion."

SATURDAY, DECEMBER 21, 1895.

London bears continue the raid on American securities, circulating wild rumors and attacking "indiscriminately and unsparingly." The entire American financial and commercial system is spoken of as rotten. The real leaders of the financial world, says the *New York Sun*, evidently decided to try the administering of a sharp touch of disaster as an object lesson against war.

Queen Victoria shows her anxiety by renewed consultations with various ministers of state.

The jocose reception of President Cleveland's message in England begins to give way to more serious consideration and less positive opposition from the press.

The House of Respresentatives responds to the President's call for financial aid and tables the holiday recess resolution; the Ways and Means Committee begins framing a bill to meet the treasury deficiency.

Evidences develop on the New York Stock Exchange of investment buying on a large scale. Banks agree to stand by sound members of the exchange. Bears in London, toward the close of the market, begin to buy in; their demand advances prices two or three points. Foreign arbitrage houses in New York continue buying from the time the market opens. Evidences are palpable in Throgmorton Street, London, that the panic is artificial. In New York the largest dealing is in Industrials which have no foreign holders. The efforts to depress stocks show signs of exhaustion about 2 o'clock. The news that Congress will take immediate action on the relief of the treasury aids the settling tendency of the market.

The *Paris Temps* prints a despatch from Rome saying the Emperor of Italy offers to arbitrate between Great Britain and the United States.

San Francisco bankers and capitalists do not respond to the panic.

General Cabell of the Trans-Mississippi Department of the Confederate Veterans telegraphs to Secretary Lamont an offer of 50,000 men in case of war.

President Cleveland signs the Venezuelan Commission Bill.

Government organs in Germany attack President Cleveland's attitude. Others, opposing the message, rejoice at its rebuke of the "world-wide arrogance of England."

The *Westminster Gazette* hopes England will make it clear that she is not attacking the Monroe Doctrine or seeking to raise that issue.

Vice-President Stevenson lays before the Senate the following resolution from both houses of the Brazilian congress :

"The Federal Senate of the United States of Brazil sends its greeting to the Senate of the United States of America upon the worthy message of President Cleveland, who so strenuously guards the dignity, the sovereignty, and the freedom of the American nations."

A London trade organization known as the Baltic cheers " Yankee Doodle."

Women at the Pilgrim Mothers' banquet, in New York, speak for peace.

The London Peace Society arranges for Sunday sermons in over one hundred pulpits urging peace at all times.

SUNDAY, DECEMBER 22, 1895.

London ministers preach peace in many pulpits at the invitation of the Peace Society.

Many American pulpits oppose war and hasty proceedings in the Venezuelan matter.

Brokers in New York become much concerned over failure to receive their customary cable advices from London.

The largest assemblage of bankers, brokers and capitalists since the Baring failure in 1890 is held in the Windsor Hotel, New York. A number of leading bank presidents hold an informal meeting in the evening.

St. Louis decides to organize a local naval company.

A Russian priest in Samokin says American Russians would take arms against England in the event of war.

Gold is reported to be coming in great quantities into the sub-treasury at Cincinnati.

President Harper of Chicago University sustains President Cleveland in vigorous language.

Ministers at Cleveland, Ohio, sustain the President.

MONDAY, DECEMBER 23, 1895.

Orders from the continent for purchases of American securities surprise the London market. London does not buy on its own account. An American banker in London advises Engligh people not to believe the financial excitement has repressed the American war spirit, for the American people, he says, wou'd rather fight thar not if it comes to a question of making a test case of upholding the Monroe Doctrine. The London stock market fluctuates all day, but at the close of the Exchange there is an utter absence of excitement. In Manchester there is a decided upward movement of stocks, American railroad securities averaging 3 per cent. higher than on Saturday. Liverpool and Glasgow Exchanges also become steady.

The New York Clearing House announces its readiness to issue loan certificates. Stocks immediately advance. London hears of the action before Wall street does and bids above the closing prices of Saturday. By noon the prices of stocks in New York gain 3 to 5 points. Philadelphia responds to the general improvement. Grain and cotton go up, English buyers contributing to the movement. The New York Clearing house action brings private bankers into the loan market. Call money closes at 5 per cent.

Actual purchases of stocks become a feature of the day in New York, and the floating supply of stocks materially diminishes. Many sales aggregate less than a hundred shares.

Comparatively little business responds to a high sterling exchange rate of $4.90½.

The Chicago Board of Trade sends a telegram to speaker Reed congratulating the House of Representatives on its "prompt and patriotic action" to relieve the treasury.

A "peace meeting" called in Cooper Union, New York, breaks up in confusion.

English papers express the opinion that America "has righted itself from unwisdom to wisdom in a night." They are disposed to think England will exterd all possible courtesies to the Venezuelan Commission.

Representative Dalzell introduces a joint resolution into the House providing $1,500,000 for a reserve supply of projectiles for the navy.

Tammany Hall, New York, passes a resolution in support of President Cleveland's Venezuelan message.

A resolution against the Venezuelan message is hissed in the Chicago Labor Congress. In the New Englanders' dinner in New York every reference to the Monroe Doctrine is cheered.

The Memphis Cotton Exchange advises farmers against planting cotton, in view of the remote possibility of war.

The Chicago Iroquois club passes strong resolutions in support of President Cleveland.

TUESDAY, DECEMBER 24, 1895.

Venezuela prepares for a grand demonstration on Christmas in honor of the United States. Panama gives a magnificent demonstration on the 23d in appreciation of Cleveland's Venezuelan message. The Mexican press speaks unanimously in support of the Monroe Doctrine.

The Senate unanimously passes a bill presented by Senator Hill of New York repealing the Confederate Disability Act.

Senator Allen of Nebraska introduces a bill providing for the establishment of a Pan-American union.

New York, Boston, Philadelphia and Chicago report improving conditions on the exchanges. Money rates are holding low. High sterling exchange is not promoting exports of gold.

London and Paris are strengthening in Americans on the stock exchanges.

FRIDAY, DECEMBER 27, 1895.

Mining stocks are again in full activity on the Denver Mining Exchange.

THE BOUNDARY DISPUTE.

The Claims of Great Britain and the Concescessions of Venezuela.

The boundary dispute between Great Britain and Venezuela is one of long standing, and dates back to the cession of Guiana to Great Britain by Holland in 1814. Years of fruitless negotiations were followed in 1887 by the rupture of diplomatic relations between the two countries.

Venezuela was discovered by Christopher Columbus July 31, 1498, on his third voyage to America, and the first landing of Spaniards was made in 1510. The country continued under Spanish rule until 1810, when the people rose to throw off the foreign yoke under the leadership of Simon Bolivar, the Washington of South America. It was in Caracas that the movement for South American freedom originated. Although independence was assured by the victory of 1821 and the Spanish army withdrew in 1823, it was not until the peace of Madrid in 1847, that Spain formally acknowledged the independence of the republic of Venezuela.

After the war of independence, or in 1822, Venezuela succeeded to the rights of Spain in territory west of the Esse-

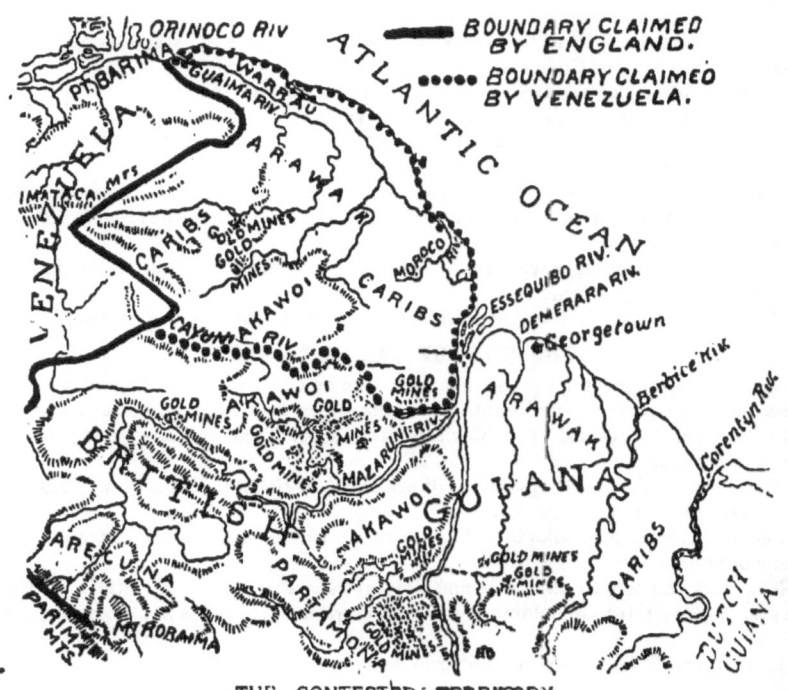

THE CONTESTED TERRITORY.

uibo river, and has always persistently
claimed it. Great Britain, of course,
must base her claims, primarily, at least,
at those of Holland before her.

The province of Guiana, forming a
part of the captaincy-general of Caracas
and pertaining to Spain, was originally
bounded on the east by the Atlantic
ocean and on the south by the Amazon
river. During the long war waged by
the Dutch to liberate themselves from
Spanish dominion, they occupied and suc-
essfully held Essequibo, Demerara and
urinam within this province of Guiana,
which places, by the treaty of Munster, in
648, were confirmed to the government
of the Netherlands. The Dutch, in viola-
tion of the terms of this treaty, made
excursions into Spanish Guiana, but were
invariably opposed by the Spanish forces.
That they never considered themselves
the legitimate owners of any of the territory west of the Essequibo river is apparent from the fact that, in the cession
of these places to Great Britain, made
n 1814, they simply transferred their
colonies of Essequibo, Demerara and
Serbice, without designating any fixed
boundary lines.

NGLAND'S EARLY ASSERTIONS.

The earliest assertions of Great
Britain to dominion beyond the Esse-
uibo were vague and hesitating. They
were based on representations that the
Dutch settlements had spread into that
region and that treaties had been exe-
uted with the Indians entitling the English to lands of comprehensive extent.
To these arguments it was replied that
the original title was vested in Spain by
virtue of discovery, and sovereignty;
that it had never been alienated or relin-
quished in any manner, and that it
passed directly to Venezuela.

Thus the case stood until Sir Robert
Schomburg drew his "arbitrary line" of
demarkation in 1841. He set up posts to
indicate British dominion at Point Bar-
ia, Amacuro and other localities. Thereupon the Venezuelan government made
vigorous protest and Lord Aberdeen
omptly ordered the posts removed.
Aberdeen was so far from urging extraordinary claims that in 1844 he spon-
aneously proposed to Dr. Fortique,
enezuelan plentipotentiary in London,
boundary line known as the "Aber-
een boundary line."

This Aberdeen proposition of 1844
as the first specific definition of Eng-
nd's patented rights, the foundation

for it in international law being the alle-
gation of Dutch settlement and Indian
treaties.

LOOKING TO ARBITRATION.

Nothing further was done until the
celebrated status quo of 1850 was established, whereby Great Britain agreed
not to occupy or encroach upon the territory in dispute in consideration of a similar agreement on the part of Venezuela.
From 1850 to 1886 the course of diplomatic affairs was very shifty. In 1881
Lord Granville, after rejecting compromise proposals, proposed a new line,
known as the "Granville line." In a note
accompanying this he said this left the
complete dominion of the mouth of the
Orinoco to Venezuela, which was regarded as equivalent to a formal disavowal by England of any design upon
the Boca Grande or great mouth of the
river. In 1883 (Lord Granville still being at the head of the foreign office)
overtures were made to Venezuela for
amicable arrangement of the boundary
difficulty among others. General Guzman Blanco was thereupon dispatched
to London by the republic as envoy extraordinary, with full powers to deal definitely with all these issues. For the
first time Venezuela was represented
sented at the court of St. James by a
diplomat of the highest order of ability.
Guzman Blanco, instead of dallying with
vexing and impracticable plans of boundary compromise, concentrated all his
efforts to give the controversy a new
direction—in favor of arbitration. In this
endeavor he arrived at the very verge
of brilliant success. June 18, 1875, Earl
Granville assented to the draft of a
treaty between England and Venezuela
which embraced an article providing that
any differences not adjustable by the
usual means of friendly negotiation
should be submitted "to the arbitration
of a third power, or of several powers in
amity with both countries, without re-
sorting to war," and that the result of
such arbitration should be binding upon
both governments.

This great diplomatic stroke of Guzman Blanco, absolutely bringing England
to bay on the boundary question, was,
however, immediately made of no avail
by the overturn of the Gladstone minis-
try. Lord Salisbury, who took office a
few days later, promptly rescinded the
arbitration clause of the purposed treaty.
Since that time England has persistently
declined every proposal to arbitrate the

matter, and is said to have enlarged her territorial claims and to have systematically prosecuted forcible aggrandizements.

UNDER ROSEBERY.

When Rosebery's government came in, however, less extravagant claims were made. As "especial importance" was attached "to the possession of the River Guiana by British Guiana," it will be seen that as late as 1886 the British were content to let the line exclude from their territory every part of the Orinoco mouth.

After 1886 England cast aside all pretense of recognition of Venezuela's sovereignty over the Boca Grande. Lord Salisbury, replying in 1890 to United States Minister Lincoln, indicated by implication that his government was unalterably resolved to share equally with Venezuela the control of that important region. Meantime the absorption of the interior has progressed without restraint, the manifest aim being to assert undisputed mastery over the extraordinarily rich gold districts of Yuruari. These districts lie very far away from the Schomburgk line, and considerably outside the Aberdeen line, wherefore England broadens out her claims to neutralize such inconvenient circumstances.

IMPORTANCE OF THE ORINOCO.

Extremely weighty consideration of empire and trade are wrapped up in England's resolve not to hazard by the chance of arbitration the valuable territory which she can, of course, hold indefinitely against a feeble state like Venezuela. While neither claiming nor admitting any rigid boundary line between Venezuela and her colony of British Guiana, there is one fixed point at which she purposes to originate a line, and from which she will not deviate. The point is on the coast, right at the center of the littoral of the Boca Grande, or grand mouth of the Orinoco river, where the small River Amacuro flows into the sea. Any boundary line projected southward from that point would include within British possessions the Barima arm (Brazo Barima) of the Orinoco and the whole island of Barima. Thus the essential feature of England's territorial contention is her claim to full equality with Venezuela in ownership and authority at the main mouth of the Orinoco.

The importance of this position for England is enormous, and even incalculable. It would give her the finest strategic situation on the continent of South America, with absolute control of the Orinoco and its numerous branches, connecting with the Amazon through the navigable streams of Casiquiari—a network of rivers draining about half the continent.

YURUARIAN INCIDENT.

Great Britain lays considerable stress on the "Yuruarian incident." British officers stationed in the Yuruarian district, which is beyond the Schomburgk line, were arrested by Venezuelans, but later released. For this arrest Great Britain makes demand of $60,000 "smart money." Lord Salisbury contends this is simply reparation for insult, but if the Venezuelans were in their own territory when they made the arrests they could hardly be held for damages. So the Monroe doctrine appears to be involved in the demand for damages for the Yuruarian incident.

Since Great Britain, following the negotiations of 1886, proceeded to occupy a portion of Venezuelan Guiana, which was the occasion of Venezuela dissolving diplomatic relations with Great Britain, the southern republic has been persistent in seeking the good offices of the United States. She has also steadily protested against the occupation by Great Britain.

Venezuela does not attach the least weight to the circumstance that the English have long enjoyed de facto possession of part of the disputed territory by actual occupation; she holds that this occupation is mere usurpation and invasion. Lord Salisbury, on the other hand, recently made the claim that this occupation gave Great Britain actual right, and that what might be subject for arbitration now would not be after a longer period of occupation.

OTHER BOUNDARIES.

Other boundaries of Venezuela have been settled recently by amicable methods. Since 1891 the frontier question towards Colombia has been settled by Spain, to which the matter had been referred. The boundary lines seem to have been subject to great dispute. Before the proclamation of independence the province of Caracas had already been officially called Venezuela, the meaning of which, as now clearly understood, corresponds to the whole space inclosed by the frontiers of Colombia, Brazil and British Guiana. Aided by numerous documents preserved in the national archives, however, the Spanish arbitrators were able in this dispute to pronounce an official verdict substantially in favor of Colombia. Toward Brazil the Venezuelan frontier was determined by treaty in 1859.

Elisee Reclus, the scientist, in his work on the earth and its inhabitants, in discussing the boundaries to the east, says the English have extended their acquisitions as far as the mouth of the Orinoco. "Thanks to this position at the entrance of the Orinoco," he continues, "Great Britain may hope some day to acquire the political and commercial supremacy in the whole of the delta region, facing which is the important military trading station of Trinidad. Since the days of Sir Walter Raleigh England has several times attempted to penetrate into the interior of the continent through this gateway. In the

archives of the Indies there exists a Spanish map, dated 1591, on which figures a large island in the middle of the delta with the legend, "Here are the English." In 1808 the British government occupied various points of the delta, where its farthest station, standing on a height between the Orinoco branches and the Guarafiche river, commanded both the entrance of the navigable channel and the Serpent's Mouth. This strategic point was spoken of as a future 'Gibraltar,' and although it has since been abandonded the Venezuelans want also to recover Barima island and all the coast lands as far as Maruca, near Nassau. They are also anxious to secure their gold fields on the Cuyini river from any risk of annexation. But they can hardly hope for success in a diplomatic struggle with Great Britain."—Chicago Record.

THE CORRESPONDENCE.

Secretary Olney's Letter and Lord Salisbury's Replies.

SECRETARY OLNEY'S LETTER.

His Instructions to Ambassador Bayard.

Department of State,
Washington, July 20, 1895.
His Excellency Thomas F. Bayard, etc., etc., London:

Sir—I am directed by the president to communicate to you his views upon a subject to which he has given much anxious thought, and respecting which he has not reached a conclusion without a lively sense of its great importance, as well as the sense of responsibility involved in any action now to be taken.

It is not proposed, and for present purposes is not necessary, to enter into any detailed account of the controversy between Great Britain and Venezuela respecting the western frontier of the colony of British Guiana. The dispute is of ancient date, and began at least as early as the time when Great

Britain acquired by the treaty with the Netherlands of 1814 the establishments of Demerara, Essequibo and Berbice. From that time to the present the dividing line between these "establishments" (now called British Guiana) and Venezuela has never ceased to be a subject of contention.

The claims of both parties, it must be conceded, are of a somewhat indefinite nature. On the one hand Venezuela, in every constitution of government since she became an independent state, has declared her territorial limits to be those of the captaincy-general of Venezuela in 1810, yet out of "moderation and prudence," it is said, she has contented herself with claiming the Essequibo line—the line of the Essequibo river, that is—to be the true boundary between Venezuela and British Guiana. On the other hand, at least an equal degree of indefiniteness distinguishes the claim of Great Britain. It does not seem to be asserted, for instance, that in 1814 the "establishments" then acquired by Great Britain had any clearly defined western limits which can now be identified, and which are either the limits insisted upon to-day or, being the original limits, have been the basis of legitimate territorial extensions. On the contrary, having the actual possession of a district called the Pomaron district, she apparently remained indifferent as to the exact area of the colony until 1840, when she commissioned an engineer, Sir Robert Schomburgk, to examine and lay down its boundaries. The result was the Schomburgk line, which was fixed by metes and bounds, was delineated on maps and was at first indicated on the face of the country itself by posts, monograms and other like symbols.

If it was expected that Venezuela would acquiesce in this line the expectation was doomed to speedy disappointment. Venezuela at once protested, and with such vigor and to such purpose that the line was explained to be only tentative—part of a general boundary scheme concerning Brazil and the Netherlands, as well as Venezuela, and the monuments of the line set up by Schomburgk were removed by the express order of Lord Aberdeen.

Under these circumstances it seems impossible to treat the Schomburgk line as being the boundary claimed by Great Britain as a matter of right, or as anything but a line originating in considerations of convenience and expediency.

Since 1840 various other boundary lines have from time to time been indicated by Great Britain—but all as convenient lines—lines to which Venezuela's assent has been desired, but which in no instance, it is believed, have been demanded as matter of right. Thus, neither of the parties is to-day standing for the boundary line predicated upon strict legal right, Great · Britain having formulated no such claim at all, while Venezuela insists upon the Essequibo line only as a liberal concession to her antagonist.

Several other features of the situation remain to be briefly noticed—the continuous growth of the undefined British claim, the fate of the various attempts at arbitration of the controversy and the part in the matter heretofore taken by the United States.

STEADY ENCROACHMENT.

As already seen, the exploitation of the Schomburgk line in 1840 was at once followed by the protest of Venezuela and by proceedings on the part of Great Britain, which could fairly be interpreted only as a disavowal of that line. Indeed, in addition to the facts already noticed, Lord Aberdeen himself, in 1844, proposed a line beginning at the River Morocco, a distinct abandonment of the Schomburgk line. Notwithstanding this, however, every change in the British claim since that time has moved the frontier of British Guiana further and further to the westward of the line thus proposed.

The Granville line of 1881 placed the starting point at a distance of twenty-nine miles from the Morocco, in the direction of Punta Barima. The Rosebery line of 1886 placed it west of the Guaima river, and about that time, if the British authority known as the Statesman's Year Book is to be relied upon, the area of British Guiana was suddenly enlarged by some 33,000 square miles, being stated as 76,000 square miles in 1885 and 109,000 square miles in 1887. The Salisbury line of 1890 fixed the starting point of the line in the mouth of the Amacuro, west of the Punta Barima, on the Orinoco. And finally, in 1893, a second Rosebery line carried the boundary from a point to the west of the Amacuro as far as the source of the Cumano river and the Sierra of Usupamo.

Nor have the various claims thus enumerated been claims on paper merely. An exercise of jurisdiction corresponding more or less to such claims has accompanied or followed closely upon each, and has been the more irritating and unjustifiable if, as is alleged, an agreement made in the year 1850 bound both parties to refrain from such occupation pending the settlement of the dispute.

While the British claim has been developing in the manner above described, Venezuela has made earnest and repeated efforts to have the question of boundary settled. Indeed, allowance being made for the distractions of a war of independence, and for frequent internal revolutions, it may be fairly said that Venezuela has never ceased to strive for its adjustment. It could, of course, do so only through peaceful methods, any resort to force as against its powerful adversary being out of the question. Accordingly, shortly after the drawing of the Schomburgk line, an effort was made to settle the boundary by treaty, and was apparently progressing towards a successful issue when the negotiations were brought to an end in 1844 by the death of the Venezuelan plenipotentiary.

VENEZUELA'S OFFER.

In 1848 Venezuela entered upon a period of civil commotions, which lasted for more than a quarter of a century, and the negotiations thus interrupted in 1844 were not renewed until 1876. In that year Venezuela offered to close the dispute by accepting the Morocco line proposed by Lord Aberdeen, but, without giving reasons for his refusal, Lord Granville rejected the proposal, and suggested a new line comprehending a large tract of territory all pretension to which seemed to have been abandoned by the previous action of Lord Aberdeen.

Venezuela refused to assent to it, and negotiations dragged along without result until 1882, when Venezuela concluded that the only course open to her was arbitration of the controversy. Before she had made any definite proposition, however, Great Britain took the matter in its own hands and suggested a treaty, which should determine various other questions, as well as that of the disputed boundary. The result was that a treaty was practically agreed upon with the Gladstone government in 1886, containing a general arbitration clause, under which the parties might have submitted the boundary dispute to the decision of a third power, or of several powers, in amity with both. Before the actual signing of the treaty, however, the administration of Mr. Gladstone was superseded by that of Lord Salisbury, which declined to accede to the arbitration clause of the treaty, notwithstanding the reasonable expectation of Venezuela to the contrary, based upon the premier's emphatic declaration in the House of Lords, that no serious government would think of not respecting the engagements of its predecessor.

RELATIONS SUSPENDED.

Since then Venezuela on the one side has been offering and calling for arbitration, while Great Britain on the other has responded by insisting upon the conditions that any arbitration should relate only to such of the disputed territory as lies west of a line designated by herself. As this condition seemed inadmissible to Venezuela, and as, while the negotiations were pending, new appropriations of what is claimed to be Venezuela territory continued to be made, Venezuela in 1887 suspended diplomatic relations with Great Britain, protesting "before her British majesty's government, before all civilized nations, and before the world in general, against the acts of spoliation committed to her detriment by the government of Great Britain, which she at no time and on no account will recognize as capable of altering in the least the rights which she has inherited from Spain, and respecting which she will ever be willing to 'submit to the decision of a third power."

Diplomatic relations have not since been restored, though what is claimed to be new and flagrant British aggressions forced Venezuela to resume negotiations on the boundary question in 1890, through its minister in Paris and a special envoy on that subject, and in 1893, through a confidential agent, Senor Michelena. These negotiations, however, met with the fate of other like previous negotiations, Great Britain refusing to arbitrate as to territory west of an arbitrary line drawn by herself.

SENOR MICHELENA'S MISSION.

All attempts in that direction were definitely terminated in October, 1893, when Senor Michelena filed with the foreign office the following declaration: "I perform a most strict duty in raising again in the name of the government of Venezuela a most solemn protest against the proceedings of the colony of British Guiana, constituting encroachments upon the territory of the republic and against the declaration contained in your excellency's communication that her Britannic majesty's government considers that part of the territory as pertaining to British Guiana and admits no claim to it on the part of Venezuela. In support of this protest I reproduce all the arguments presented to your excellency in my note of the 29th of last September, and those which have been exhibited by the government of Venezuela on the various occasions they have raised the same protest. I lay on her Britannic majesty's government the entire responsibility of the incidents that may arise in the future from the necessity to which Venezuela has been driven to oppose by all possible means the dispossession of a part of her territory, for by disregarding her just representation to put an end to this violent state of affairs through the decision of arbiters, her majesty's government ignores her rights and imposes upon her the painful though peremptory duty of providing for her own legitimate defense."

WE COULD NOT IGNORE IT.

To the territorial controversy between Great Britain and the republic of Venezuela, thus briefly outlined, the United States has not been and, indeed, in view of its traditional policy, could not be indifferent. The note to the British foreign office, by which Venezuela opened negotiations in 1876, was at once communicated to this government. In January, 1881, a letter of the Venezuelan minister at Washington, respecting certain alleged demonstrations at the mouth of the Orinoco, was thus answered by Mr. Evarts, then secretary of state:

In the February following Mr. Evarts wrote again on the same subject as follows:

In reply I have to inform you that in view of the deep interest which the government of the United States takes in all transactions tending to attempted encroachment of foreign powers upon the territory of any of the republics of this continent, this government could not look with indifference to the forcible acquisition of such territory by England if the mission of the vessels now at the mouth of the Orinoco should be found to be for that end. This government awaits, therefore, with natural concern the more particular statement promised by the government of Venezuela, which it hopes will not long be delayed.

Referring to your note of December 21 last touching the operations of certain British war vessels in and near the mouth of the Orinoco river, and to my reply thereto of the 31st ultimo, as well as to the recent occasions in which the subject has been mentioned in our conferences concerning the business of your mission, I take it to be fitting now, at the closing incumbency of the office I hold, to advert to the interest with which the government of the United States cannot fail to regard any such purpose with respect to the control of American territory as is stated to be contemplated by the government of Great Britain and to express my regret that the further information promised in your note with regard to such designs had not reached me in season to receive the attention which, notwithstanding the severe pressure of public business at the end of an administrative term, I should have taken pleasure in bestowing upon it. I doubt not, however, that your representations in fulfillment of the awaited additional orders of your government will have like earnest and solicitous consideration at the hands of my successor.

SECRETARY EVARTS' EFFORTS.

In November, 1882, the then state of negotiations with Great Britain, together with a copy of an intended note suggesting recourse to arbitration, was communicated to the secretary of state by the president of Venezuela, with the expression of the hope that the United States would give him its opinion and advice and such support as it deemed possible to offer Venezuela in order that justice should be done her.

FRELINGHUYSEN'S SUGGESTIONS.

Mr. Frelinghuysen replied in a dispatch to the United States minister at Caracas as follows:

This government has already expressed its view that arbitration of such dispute is a convenient resort in the case of failure to come to a mutual understanding, and intimated its willingness, if Venezuela should so desire, to propose to Great Britain such a mode of settlement. It is felt that the tender of good offices would not be so profitable if the United States were to approach Great Britain as the advocate of any prejudged solution in favor of Venezuela. So far as the United States can counsel and assist Venezuela it believes it best to confine its reply to the renewal of the suggestion, the more easily made since it appears from the instruction sent by Senor Seijas to the Venezuelan minister in London on the same 15th of July, 1882, that the president of Venezuela proposed to the British government the submission of the dispute to arbitration by a third power.

You will take an early occasion to present the foregoing considerations to Senor Seijas, saying to him that, while trusting that the direct proposal for arbitration already made to Great Britain may bear good fruit (if, indeed, it has not already done so by its acceptance in principle), the government of the United States will cheerfully lend any needful aid to press upon Great Britain in a friendly way the proposition so made; and at the same time you will say to Senor Seijas (in personal conference and not with the formality of a written communication) that the United States, while advocating strongly the recourse of arbitration for the adjustment of international disputes affecting the state of America, does not seek to put itself forward as their arbiter; that, viewing all such questions impartially and with no intent or desire to prejudice their merits, the United States will not refuse its arbitration if asked by both parties, and that, regarding all such questions as are essentially and distinctively American, the United States would always prefer to see such contention adjusted through the arbitrament of an American rather than a European power.

BLANCO'S VISIT TO LONDON.

In 1884 General Guzman Blanco, the Venezuelan minister to England, appointed with special reference to pending negotiations for a general treaty with Great Britain, visited Washington on his way to London, and after several conferences with the secretary of state respecting the objects of his mission, was thus commended to the good offices of Mr. Lowell, our minister at St. James:

It will necessarily be somewhat within your discretion how far your good offices may be profitably employed with her majesty's government to these ends, and at any rate you may take proper occasion to let Lord Granville know that we are not without concern as to whatever may affect the interests of a sister republic of the American continent, or its position in the family of nations. If General Guzman should apply to you for advice or assistance in realizing the purposes of his mission, you will show him proper consideration, and, without ommitting the United States to any determinate political solution, you will endeavor to carry out the views of this instruction.

The progress of General Guzman's negotiations did not fail to be observed by this government, and in December, 886, with a view to preventing the rupture of diplomatic relations—which actually took place in February following—he then secretary of state, Mr. Bayard, instructed our minister to Great Britain to tender the arbitration of the United States in the following terms:

It does not appear that at any time heretofore the good offices of this government have been actually tendered to avert a rupture between Great Britain and Venezuela. s intimated in my No. 58, our inaction in his regard would seem to be due to the reluctance of Venezuela to have the government of the United States take any steps having relation to the action or at would in appearance even, prejudice the resort to further arbitration or mediation which Venezuela desired. Nevertheless, the records abundantly testify our friendly concern in the adjustment of the dispute; and the intelligence now received warrants me in tendering through you to her majesty's government the good offices of the United States to promote an amicable settlement of the respective claims of Great Britain and Venezuela in the premises. As proof of the impartiality with which we view the question, we offer our arbitration, if acceptable, to both countries. We do this with the less hesitancy as the dispute turns upon simple and readily ascertainable historical facts.

Her majesty's government will readily understand that this attitude of friendly neutrality and entire impartiality touching the merits of the controversy, consisting wholly in a difference of facts between our friends and neighbors, is entirely consistent and compatible with the sense of responsibility that rests upon the United States in relation to the South American republics. The doctrines we announced two generations ago, at the instance and with the moral support and approval of the British government, have lost none of their force of importance in the progress of time, and the governments of Great Britain and the United States are equally interested in conserving a status the wisdom of which has been demonstrated by the experience of more than half a century.

It is proper, therefore, that you should convey to Lord Iddesleigh, in such sufficiently guarded terms as your discretion may dictate, the satisfaction that would be felt by the government of the United States in perceiving that its wishes in this regard were permitted to have influence with her majesty's government.

ENGLAND STILL REFUSES.

This offer of mediation was declined by Great Britain, with the statement that a similar offer had already been received from another quarter, and that the queen's government were still not without hope of a settlement by direct diplomatic negotiations.

In February, 1888, having been informed that the governor of British Guiana had by formal decree laid claim to the territory traversed by the route of a proposed railway from Ciudad Bolivar to Guacipati, Mr. Bayard addressed a note to our minister to England, from which the following extracts are taken:

The claim now stated to have been put forth by the authorities of British Guiana necessarily gives rise to grave disquietude and creates an apprehension that the territorial claim does not follow historical traditions or evidence, but is apparently indefinite. At no time hitherto does it appear that the district of which Guacipati is the center has been claimed as British territory or that such jurisdiction has ever been asserted over its inhabitants, and if the reported decree of the governor of British Guiana be indeed genuine it is not apparent how any line of railway from Ciudad Bolivar to Guacipati could enter or traverse that territory within the control of Great Britain.

It is true that the line claimed by Great Britain as the western boundary of British Guiana is uncertain and vague. It is only necessary to examine the British Colonial Office List for a few years back to perceive this. In the issue for 1877, for instance, the line runs nearly southwardly from the mouth of the Amacuro to the junction of the Cotinga and Takutu rivers. In the issue of 1887, ten years later, it makes a wide detour to the westward, following the Yuruari. Guacipati lies considerably to the westward of the line officially claimed in 1887, and it may perhaps be instructive to compare with it the map which doubtless will be found in the Colonial Office List for the present year.

It might be well for you to express anew to Lord Salisbury the great gratification it would afford this government to see the Venezuelan disputes amicably and honorably settled by arbitration or otherwise, and our readiness to do anything we properly can to assist to that end. In the course of your conversation you may refer to the publication in the London Financier of January 24 (a copy of which you can procure and exhibit to Lord Salisbury), and express apprehension lest the widening of pretensions of British Guiana to possess territory over which Venezuela's jurisdiction has never heretofore been disputed, may not diminish the chances for a practical settlement.

If, indeed, it should appear that there is no fixed limit to the British boundary claim, our good disposition to aid in a settlement might not only be defeated, but be obliged to give place to a feeling of grave concern.

BLAINE ALSO FAILED.

In 1889 information having been received that Barima, at the mouth of the Orinoco, had been declared a British port, Mr. Blaine, then secretary of state, authorized Mr. White to confer with Lord Salisbury for the re-establishment of diplomatic relations between Great Britain and Venezuela on the basis of a temporary restoration of the status quo, and on May 1 and May 6, 1890, sent the following telegrams to our minister to England, Mr. Lincoln:

May, 1, 1890.

Mr. Lincoln is instructed to use his good offices with Lord Salisbury to bring about the resumption of diplomatic intercourse between Great Britain and Venezuela as a preliminary step towards the settlement of the boundary dispute by arbitration. The joint proposals of Great Britain and the United States towards Portugal, which have just been brought about, would seem to make the present time propitious for submitting this question to the international arbitration. He is requested to propose to Lord Salisbury, with a view to an accommodation, that an informal conference be had in Washington or in London of representatives of three powers. In such conference the position of the United States is one solely of impartial friendship towards both litigants.

May 6, 1890.

It is, nevertheless, desired that you shall do all you can consistently with our attitude of impartial friendship to induce some accord between the contestants by which the merits of the controversy may be fairly ascertained and the rights of each party justly confirmed. The neutral position of this government does not comport with any expression of opinion on the part of this department as to what these rights are, but it is confident that the shifting feeling on which the British boundary question has rested for several years past is an obstacle to such a correct appreciation of the nature and grounds of her claim as would alone warrant the formation of any opinion.

VENEZUELA SENDS AN ENVOY.

In the course of the same year, 1890, Venezuela sent to London a special envoy to bring about the resumption of diplomatic relations with Great Britain through the good offices of the United States minister. But the mission failed because a condition of such resumption, steadily adhered to by Venezuela, was the reference of the boundary dispute to arbitration. Since the close of the negotiations initiated by Senor Michelena in 1893, Venezuela has repeatedly brought the controversy to the notice of the United States; has insisted upon its importance to the United States as well as to Venezuela; has represented it to have reached an acute stage making the limit action by the United States imperative, and has not ceased to solicit the services and support of the United States in aid of its final adjustment. These appeals have not been received with indifference, and our ambassador to Great Britain has been uniformly instructed to exert all his influence in the direction of the reestablishment of diplomatic relations between Great Britain and Venezuela and in favor of arbitration of the boundary controversy.

The secretary of state, in a communication to Mr. Bayard, bearing date July 13, 1894, used the following language:

The president is inspired by a desire for peaceable and honorable settlement of th[e] existing difficulties between an America[n] state and a powerful transatlantic natio[n] and would be glad to see the re-establish[-] ment of such diplomatic relations betwee[n] them as would promote that end. I can dis[-] cern but two equitable solutions of the pres[-] ent controversy. One is the arbitral deter[-] mination of the rights of the disputants a[s] the respective successors to the historica[l] rights of Holland and Spain over the region in question. The other is to create [a] new boundary line in accordance with th[e] dictates of mutual expediency and consider[-] ation. The two governments have so fa[r] been unable to agree on a conventiona[l] line. The consistent and conspicuous advo[-] cacy by the United States and England o[f] the principle of arbitration, and their re[-] course thereto in settlement of importan[t] questions arising between them, makes suc[h] a mode of adjustment especially appropriat[e] in the present instance, and this govern[-] ment will gladly do what it can to furthe[r] a determination in that sense.

Subsequent communications to Mr. Bayard direct him to ascertain whether a minister from Venezuela would be received by Great Britain.

CLEVELAND LAST DECEMBER.

In the annual message to Congress of December 3 last, the president used the following language:

The boundary of British Guiana still remains in dispute between Great Britain an[d] Venezuela. Believing that its early settle[-] ment, on some just basis alike honorable to both parties, is in the line of our establishe[d] policy to remove from this hemisphere a[ll] causes of difference with powers beyond th[e] sea, I shall renew the efforts heretofor[e] made to bring about a restoration of diplo[-] matic relations between the disputants an[d] to induce a reference to arbitration, a resor[t] which Great Britain so conspicuously favor[s] in principle and respects in practice, an[d] which is earnestly sought by her weake[r] adversary.

And February 22, 1895, a joint reso[-] tion of Congress declared;

That the president's suggestion that Grea[t] Britain and Venezuela refer their disput[e] as to boundaries to friendly arbitration b[e] earnestly recommended to the favorable consideration of both parties in interest.

The important features of the existing situation, as shown by the foregoing, may be briefly stated. The title to territory of indefinite but confessedly very large extent is in dispute between Great Britain on the one hand and the South American republic of Venezuela on the other. The disparity in the strength of the claimants is such that Venezuela can hope to establish her claim only through peaceful methods— through an agreement with her adversary, either upon the subject itself or upon an arbitration. The controversy, with varying claims on the part of Great Britain, has existed for more than half a century, during which period many earnest and persistent efforts of Venezuela to establish a boundary by agreement have proved unsuccessful. The futility of the endeavor to obtain a conventional line being recognized, Venezuela for a quarter of a century has asked and striven for arbitration. Great Britain, however, has always and continuously refused to arbitrate, except upon the condition of a renunciation of a large part of the Venezuelan claim and of a concession to herself of a large share of the territory in controversy.

By the frequent interposition of its good offices at the instance of Venezuela, by constantly urging and promoting the restoration of diplomatic relations between the two countries by pressing for arbitration of the disputed boundary, by offering to act as arbitrator, by expressing its grave concern whenever new alleged instances of British aggression upon Venezuelan territory have been brought to its notice, the government of the United States has made it clear to Great Britain and to the world that the controversy is one in which its honor and interests are involved, and the continuance of which it cannot regard with indifference.

AMERICA'S INTEREST.

The accuracy of the foregoing analysis of the existing status cannot, it is believed, be challenged. It shows that status to be such that those charged with the interests of the United States are now forced to determine exactly what those interests are and what course of action they require. It compels them to decide to what extent, if any, the United States may and should intervene in a controversy between and primarily concerning only Great Britain and Venezuela, and to see how far it is bound to see that the integrity of Venezuelan territory is not impaired by the pretensions of its powerful antagonist.

Are any such right and duty devolved upon the United States? If not, the United States has already done all, if not more than all, that a purely sentimental interest in the affairs of the two countries justifies, and to push its interposition farther would be unbecoming and undignified, and might well subject it to the charge of impertinent interference with affairs with which it has no rightful concern. On the other hand, if any such right and duty exist, their due exercise and discharge will not permit of any action that shall not be efficient and that, if the power of the United

States is adequate, shall not result in the accomplishment of the end in view. The question thus presented, as matter of principle, and regard being had to the settled national policy, does not seem difficult of solution. Let such momentous practical consequences depend on its determination that it should be carefully considered and that the grounds of the conclusion arrived at should be fully and frankly stated.

That there are circumstances under which a nation may justly interpose in a controversy to which two or more other nations are the direct and immediate parties, is an admitted canon of international law. The doctrine is ordinarily expressed in terms of the most general character, and is, perhaps, incapable of more specific statement. It is declared in substance that a nation may avail itself of this right whenever what is done or proposed by any of the parties primarily concerned is a serious and direct menace to its own integrity, tranquility or welfare. The propriety of the rule, when applied in good faith, will not be questioned in any quarter. On the other hand, it is an inevitable though unfortunate consequence of the wide scope of the rule that it has only too often been made a cloak for schemes of wanton spoliation and aggrandizement.

WASHINGTON'S FAREWELL.

We are concerned at this time, however, not so much with the general rule as with a form of it which is peculiarly and distinctively American. Washington, in the solemn admonitions of his farewell address, explicitly warned his countrymen against entanglements with the politics or the controversies of European powers. "Europe," he said, "has a set of primary interests which to us have none—or a very remote—relation. Hence she must be engaged in frequent controversies, the causes of which are essentially foreign to our concerns. Hence, therefore, it must be unwise in us to implicate ourselves by artificial ties in the ordinary vicissitudes of her politics or the ordinary combinations and collisions of her friendships or enmities. Our detached and distant situation invites and enables us to pursue a different course."

During the administration of President Monroe this doctrine of the farewell address was first considered in all its aspects and with a view to all its practical consequences. The farewell address, while it took America out of the field of European politics, was silent as to the part Europe might be permitted to play in America. Doubtless it was thought the latest addition to the family of nations should not make haste to prescribe rules for the guidance of older members, and the expediency and propriety of serving the powers of Europe with notice of a complete and distinctive American policy, excluding them from interference with American political affairs, might well seem dubious to a generation to whom the French alliance, with its manifold advantage to the cause of American independence was fresh in mind.

TWENTY YEARS LATER.

Twenty years later, however, the situation had changed. The lately born nation had greatly increased in power and resources, had demonstrated its strength on land and sea, as well in the conflicts of arms as in the pursuits of peace, and had begun to realize the commanding position on this continent which the character of its people, their free institutions, and their remoteness from the chief scene of European contentions combined to give it. The Monroe administration, therefore, did not hesitate to accept and apply the logic of the farewell address, by declaring in effect that American non-intervention in European affairs necessarily implied and meant European non-intervention in American affairs. Conceiving, unquestionably, that complete European non-interference in American concerns would be cheaply purchased by complete American non-interference in European concerns, President Monroe, in the celebrated message of December 2, 1823, used the following language:

In the wars of the European powers in matters relating to themselves we have never taken any part, nor does it comport with our policy to do so. It is only when our rights are invaded or seriously menaced that we resent injuries or make preparations for our defense. With the movements in this hemisphere we are, of necessity, more immediately connected, and by causes which must be obvious to all enlightened and impartial observers. The political system of the allied powers is essentially different in this respect from that of America. This difference proceeds from that which exists in their respective governments; and to the defense of our own, which has been achieved by the loss of so much blood and treasure and matured by the wisdom of our most enlightened citizens, and under which we have enjoyed unexampled felicity, this whole nation is devoted. We owe it, therefore, to candor and to the amicable relations existing between the United States and these powers to declare that we should consider any attempt on their part to extend their system to any portion of this hemisphere as dangerous to our peace and safety.

With the existing colonies or dependencies of any European power we have not interfered and shall not interfere, but with the governments who have declared their independence and maintained it, and whose independence we have, on great consideration and on just principles, acknowledged, we could not view any interposition for the purpose of oppressing them, or controlling in any other manner their destiny by any European power in any other light than as the manifestation of an unfriendly disposition towards the United States.

Our policy in regard to Europe, which was adopted at an early stage of the wars which have so long agitated that quarter of the globe, nevertheless remains the same, which is, not to interfere in the internal concerns of any of its powers; to consider the government de facto as the legitimate government for us; to cultivate friendly relations with it, and to preserve those relations by a frank, firm and manly policy, meeting, in all instances, the just claims of every power, submitting to injuries from none.

But in regard to these continents circumstances are eminently and conspicuously different. It is impossible that the allied powers should extend their political system to any portion of either continent without endangering our peace and happiness, nor can any one believe that our southern brethren, if left to themselves, would adopt it of their own accord. It is equally impossible, therefore, that we should behold such interposition in any form with indifference.

SERVED NOTICE ON EUROPE.

The Monroe administration, however, did not content itself with formulating a correct rule for the regulation of the relations between Europe and America. It aimed at also securing the practical benefits to result from the application of the rule. Hence the message just quoted declared that the American continents were fully occupied and were not the subjects for future colonization by European powers. To this spirit and this purpose, also, are to be attributed the passages of the same message which treat any infringement of the rule against interference in American affairs on the part of the powers of Europe as an act of unfriendliness to the United States. It was realized that it was futile to lay down such a rule unless its observance could be enforced. It was manifest that the United States was the only power in this hemisphere capable of enforcing it. It was, therefore, courageously declared not merely that Europe ought not to interfere in American affairs, but that any European power doing so would be regarded as antagonizing the interests and inviting the opposition of the United States.

That America is in no part open to colonization, though the proposition was not universally admitted at the time of its first enunciation, has long been universally conceded. We are now concerned, therefore, only with that other practical application of the Monroe doctrine, the disregard of which by a European power is to be deemed an act of unfriendliness towards the United States. The precise scope and limitations of this rule cannot be too clearly apprehended. It does not establish any general protectorate by the United States over other American states. It does not relieve any American state from its obligations as fixed by international law, nor prevent any European power directly interested from enforcing such obligations or from inflicting merited punishment for the breach of them.

It does not contemplate any interference in the internal affairs of any American state or in the relations between it and other American states. It does not justify any attempt on our part to change the established form of government of any American state or to prevent the people of such state from altering that form according to their own will and pleasure. The rule in question has but a single purpose and object. It is that no European power or combination of European powers shall forcibly deprive an American state of the right and power of self-government and of shaping for itself its own political fortunes and destinies.

ACCEPTED LAW OF THE COUNTRY.

That the rule thus defined has been the accepted public law of this country ever since its promulgation cannot fairly be denied. Its pronouncement by the Monroe administration at that particular time was unquestionably due to the inspiration of Great Britain, who at once gave it an open and unqualified adhesion, which has never been withdrawn. But the rule was decided upon and formulated by the Monroe administration as a distinctively American doctrine, of great import to the safety and welfare of the United States, after the most careful consideration by a cabinet which numbered among its members John Quincy Adams, Calhoun, Crawford and Wirt, and which, before acting, took both Jefferson and Madison into its counsels. Its promulgation was received with acclaim by the entire people of the country, irrespective of party.

Three years after Webster declared that the doctrine involved the honor of the country. "I look upon it," he said,

"as part of its treasures of reputation, and for one I intend to guard it." And, he added, "I look on the message of December, 1823, as forming a bright page in our history. I will help neither to erase it nor to tear it out; nor shall it be by any act of mine blurred or blotted. It did honor to the sagacity of the government, and I will not diminish that honor."

Though the rule thus highly eulogized by Webster has never been formally affirmed by Congress, the House in 1864 declared against the Mexican monarchy sought to be set up by the French as not in accord with the policy of the United States, and in 1889 the Senate expressed its disapproval of the connection of any European power with a canal across the Isthmus of Darien or Central America. It is manifest that if a rule has been openly and uniformly declared and acted upon by the executive branch of the government for more than seventy years without express repudiation by Congress it must be conclusively presumed to have its sanction. Yet it is certainly no more than the exact truth to say that every administration since President Monroe's has had occasion, and sometimes more occasions than one, to examine and consider the Monroe doctrine, and has in each instance given it emphatic endorsement. Presidents have dwelt upon it in messages to Congress, and secretaries of state have time after time made it the theme of diplomatic representation.

PRACTICAL RESULTS.

Nor, if the practical results of the rule be sought for, is the record either meagre or obscure. Its first and immediate effect was indeed more momentous and far-reaching. It was the controlling factor in the emancipation of South America, and to it the independent states which now divide that region between them are largely indebted for their very existence. Since then the most striking single achievement to be credited to the rule is the evacuation of Mexico by the French upon the termination of the civil war. But we are also indebted to it for the provisions of the Clayton-Bulwer treaty, which both neutralized any interoceanic canal across Central America and expressly excluded Great Britain from occupying or exercising any dominion over any part of Central America. It has been used in the case of Cuba, as if justifying the position that, while the sovereignty of Spain will be respected, the island will not be permitted to become the possession of any other European power. It has been influential in bringing about the definite relinquishment of any supposed protectorate by Great Britain over the Mosquito coast.

President Polk, in the case of Yucatan and the proposed voluntary transfer of that country to Great Britain or Spain, relied upon the Monroe doctrine, though perhaps erroneously, when he declared in a special message to congress on the subject that the United States could not consent to any such transfer. Yet, in somewhat the same spirit, Secretary Fish affirmed in 1870 that President Grant had but followed "the teachings of all our history" in declaring in his annual message of that year that existing dependencies were no longer regarded as subject to transfer from one European power to another, and that when the present relation of colonies ceases they are to become independent powers.

Another development of the rule, though apparently not necessarily required by either its letter or its spirit, is found in the objection to arbitration of South American controversies by a European power. American questions, it is said, are for American decision, and on that ground the United States went so far as to refuse to mediate in the war between Chili and Peru jointly with Great Britain and France.

Finally, on the ground, among others, that the authority of the Monroe doctrine and the prestige of the United States as its exponent and sponsor would be seriously impaired, Secretary Bayard strenuously resisted the enforcement of the Pelletir claim against Hayti.

HOW MR. BAYARD UPHELD IT.

"The United States," he said, "has proclaimed herself the protector of this western world, in which she is by far the stronger power, from the intrusion of European sovereignties. She can point with proud satisfaction to the fact that over and over again has she declared effectively that serious indeed would be the consequences if European hostile foot should, without just cause, tread those states in the new world which have emancipated themselves from European control. She has announced that she would cherish, as it becomes her, the territorial rights of the feeblest of those states, regarding them not merely as in the eye of the law equal to even the greatest of nationalities, but in view of her distinctive policy as entitled to be regarded by her as the objects of a peculiarly gracious care. I feel bound to say that if we should sanction by reprisals in Hayti the ruthless invasion of her territory and insult to her sovereignty which the facts now before us disclose, if we approve by solemn executive action and congressional assent that invasion, it would be difficult for us hereafter to assert that in the new world, of whose rights we are the peculiar guardians, these rights have never been invaded by ourselves."

The foregoing enumeration not only shows the many instances wherein the rule in question has been affirmed and applied, but also demonstrates that the Venezuelan boundary controversy is in any view far within the scope and spirit of the rule as uniformly accepted and acted upon. A doctrine of American public law thus long and firmly established and supported could not easily be ignored in a proper case for its application, even were the considerations upon which it is founded obscure or questionable. No such objection can be made, however, to the Monroe doctrine understood and defined in the manner already stated. It rests, on the contrary, upon facts and principles that are both intelligible and incontrovertible.

NO INTEREST IN EUROPE.

That distance and three thousand miles of intervening ocean make any permanent political union between a European and an American state unnatural and inexpedient will hardly be denied. But physical and geographical considerations are the least of the objections to such a union. Europe, as Washington observed, has a set of primary interests which are peculiar to herself. America is not interested in them and ought not to be vexed or complicated with them. Each great European power, for instance, to-day maintains enormous armies and fleets in self-defense and for protection against any other European power or powers. What have the states of America to do with that condition of things, or why should they be impoverished by wars or preparations for wars with whose causes or results they can have no direct concern? If all Europe were suddenly to fly to arms over the fate of Turkey, would it not be preposterous that any American state should find itself inextricably involved in the miseries and burdens of the contest? If it were it would have to be a partner in the cost and losses of the struggle, but not in any ensuing benefits.

What is true of the material is no less true of what may be termed the moral interests involved. Those pertaining to Europe are peculiar to her, and are entirely diverse from those pertaining and peculiar to America. Europe as a whole is monarchical, and, with the single important exception of the republic of France, is committed to the monarchical principle. America, on the other hand, is devoted to the exactly opposite principle—to the idea that every people has an inalienable right of self-government, and in the United States of America has furnished to the world the most conspicuous and conclusive example and proof of the excellence of free institutions, whether from the standpoint of national greatness or of individual happiness.

INCONGRUOUS AND INJURIOUS.

It cannot be necessary, however, to enlarge upon this phase of the subject. Whether moral or material interests be considered, it cannot but be universally conceded that those of Europe are irreconcilably diverse from those of America, and that any European control of the latter is necessarily both incongruous and injurious.

If, however, for the reasons stated, the forcible intrusion of European powers into American politics is to be deprecated; if, as it is to be deprecated, it should be resisted and prevented, such resistance and prevention must come from the United States. They would come from it, of course, were it made the point of attack, but if they come at all they must also come from it when any other American state is attacked, since only the United States has the strength adequate to the exigency. Is it true, then, that the safety and welfare of the United States are so coincident with the maintenance of the independence of every American state as against every European power as to justify and require the interposition of the United States whenever that independence is endangered? The question can be candidly answered in but one way.

NATURAL ALLIES.

The states of America, South as well as North, by geographical proximity, by natural sympathy, by similarity of governmental constitutions, are friends and allies, commercially and politically, of the United States. To allow the subjugation of any of them by a European power is, of course, to completely reverse that situation, and signifies the loss of all the advantages incident to their natural relations to us.

But that is not all. The people of the United States have a vital interest in the cause of popular self-government. They have secured the right for themselves and their posterity at the cost of infinite blood and treasure. They have realized and exemplified its beneficial operation by a career unexampled in point of national greatness or individual felicity. They believe it to be for the healing of all nations, and that civilization must either advance or retrograde accordingly as its supremacy is extended or curtailed.

Imbued with these sentiments, the people of the United States might not impossibly be wrought up to an active propaganda in favor of a cause so highly valued by themselves and for mankind. But the age of the crusader has passed and they are content with such assertions and defense of the right of popular self-government as their own security and welfare demand. It is in that view more than in any other that they believe it not to be tolerated that the political control of an American state shall be forcibly assumed by a European power. The mischiefs apprehended from such a source are none the less real because not immediately imminent in any specific case, and are none the less to be guarded against because the combination of circumstances that will bring them upon us cannot be predicted.

The civilized states of Christendom deal with each other on substantially the same principles that regulate the conduct of individuals. The greater its enlightenment the more surely every state perceives that its permanent interests require it to be governed by the immutable principles of right and justice. Each, nevertheless, is only too liable to succumb to the temptations offered by seeming special opportunities for its own aggrandizement, and each would rashly imperil its own safety were it not to remember that for the regard and respect of other states it must be largely dependent upon its own strength and power.

SUPREME ON THIS CONTINENT.

To-day the United States is practically sovereign on this continent, and its fiat is law upon the subjects to which it confines its interposition. Why? It is not because of the pure friendship or good will felt for it. It is not simply by reason of its high character as a civilized state, nor because wisdom and justice and equity are the invariable characteristics of the dealings of the United States. It is because, in addition to all other grounds, its infinite resources, combined with its isolated position, render it master of the situation and practically invulnerable as against any or all other powers. All the advantages of this superiority are at once imperilled if the principle be admitted that European powers may convert American states into colonies or provinces of their own. The principle would be eagerly availed of, and every power doing so would immediately acquire a base of military operations against us. What one power was permitted to do could not be denied to another, and it is not inconceivable that the struggle now going on for the acquisition of Africa might be transferred to South America. If it were, the weaker countries would unquestionably be soon absorbed, while the ultimate result might be the partition of all South America between the various European powers.

The disastrous consequences to the United States of such a condition of things are obvious. The loss of prestige, of authority, and of weight in the councils of the family of nations would be among the least of these. Our only real rivals in peace as well as enemies in war would be located at our very doors. Thus far in our history we have been spared the burdens and evils of immense standing armies and all the other accessories of hugh warlike establishments, and the exemption has largely contributed to our national greatness and wealth as well as to the happiness of every citizen. But with the powers of Europe permanently encamped on American soil, the ideal conditions we have thus far enjoyed cannot be expected to continue. We, too, must be armed to the teeth; we, too, must convert the flower of our male population into soldiers and sailors, and by withdrawing them from the various pursuits of peaceful industry, we, too, must practically annihilate a large share of the productive energy of the nation. How a greater calamity than this could overtake us, it is difficult to see.

FRIENDSHIP NO SECURITY.

Nor are our just apprehensions to be allayed by the suggestions of the friendliness of European powers, of their good will, of their disposition, should they be our neighbors, to dwell with us in peace and harmony. The people of the United States have learned in the school of experience to what extent the retaliations

of states to each other depend not upon sentiment nor principle, but upon selfish interest. They will not soon forget that in their hour of distress, all their anxieties and burdens were aggravated by the possibility of demonstrations against their national life on the part of powers with whom they had long maintained the most harmonious relations. They have yet in mind that France seized upon the apparent opportunity of our civil war to set up a monarchy in the adjoining state of Mexico. They realize that had France and Great Britain held important South American possessions to work from and to benefit, the temptation to destroy the predominance of the great republic in this hemisphere by furthering its dismemberment might have been irresistible. From that grave peril they have been saved in the past, and may be saved again in the future through the operation of the sure but silent force of the doctrine proclaimed by President Monroe. To abandon it on the other hand, disregarding both the logic of the situation and the fact of our past experience, would be to renounce a policy which has proved both an easy defense against foreign aggression and a prolific source of internal progress and prosperity.

AS APPLIED TO VENEZUELA.

There is, then, a doctrine of American public law, well founded in principle and abundantly sanctioned by precedent which entitles and requires the United States to treat as an injury to itself the the forcible assumption by a European power of political control over an American state. The application of the doctrine to the boundary dispute between Great Britain and Venezuela remains to be made and presents no real difficulty. Though the dispute relates to a boundary line, yet, as it is between states, it necessarily imports political control to be lost by one party and gained by the other. The political control at stake, too, is of no mean importance, but concerns a domain of great extent. The British claim, it will be remembered apparently expanded in two years some 33,000 square miles, and, if it also directly involves the command of the mouth of the Orinoco, is of immense consequence in connection with the whole river navigation of the interior of South America.

It has been intimated, indeed, that in respect of these South American possessions Great Britain is herself an Amer can state, like any other, so that a controversy between her and Venezuela is to be settled between themselves as if it were between Venezuela and Brazil, or between Venezuela and Colombia, and does not call for or justify United States intervention. If this view be tenable at all the logical sequence is plain. Great Britain, as a South American state, is to be entirely differentiated from Great Britain generally, and if the boundary question cannot be settled otherwise than by force, British Guiana with her own independent resources, and not those of the British empire, should be left to settle the matter with Venezuela—an arrangement which very possibly Venezuela might not object to.

NOT AN AMERICAN POWER.

But the proposition that a European power with an American dependency is for the purposes of the Monroe doctrine to be classed not as a European but as an American state will not admit of serious discussion. If it were to be adopted the Monroe doctrine would be too valueless to be worth asserting. Not only would every European power now having a South American colony be enabled to extend its possessions on this continent indefinitely, but any other European power might also do the same by first taking pains to procure a fraction of South American soil by voluntary cession. The declaration of the Monroe message that existing colonies or dependencies of a European power would not be interfered with by the United States means colonies or dependencies then existing, with their limits as then existing. So it has been invariably construed, and so it must continue to be construed, unless it is to be deprived of all vital force. Great Britain cannot be deemed a South American state within the purview of the Monroe doctrine, nor, if she is appropriating Venezuelan territory, is it material that she does so by advancing the frontier of an old colony instead of by the planting of a new colony. The difference is a matter of form and not of substance, and the doctrine, if pertinent in the one case, must be in the other also.

It is not admitted, however, and therefore cannot be assumed, that Great Britain is in fact usurping dominion over Venezuelan territory. While Venezuela charges such usurpations, Great Britain denies it, and the United States, until the merits are authoritatively ascertained, can take sides with neither. But while this is so, while the United States may not, under existing circumstances, at least, take upon itself to say which of the two parties is right and which wrong, it is certainly within its right to demand that the truth shall be ascertained. Being entitled to resent and resist any sequestration of Venezuelan soil by Great Britain, it is necessarily entitled to know whether such sequestration has occurred or is now going on. Otherwise, if the United States is without the right to know and have it determined whether there is or is not British aggression upon Venezuelan territory, its right to protest against or repel such aggression may be dismissed from consideration. The right to act upon a fact, the existence of which there is no right to have ascertained, is simply illusory.

PEACEFUL ARBITRATION.

It being clear, therefore, that the United States may legitimately insist upon the merits of the boundary question being determined, it is equally clear that there is but one feasible mode of determining them, viz., peaceful arbitration. The impracticability of any conventional adjustment has been often and thoroughly demonstrated. Even more impossible of consideration is an appeal to arms, a mode of settling national pretensions unhappily not yet wholly obsolete. If, however, it were not condemnable as a relic of barbarism and a crime in itself, so one-sided a contest could not be invited, nor even accepted by Great Britain without distinct disparagement to her character as a civilized State.

Great Britain, however, assumes no such attitude. On the contrary, she both admits that there is a controversy and that arbitration should be resorted to for its adjustment. But, while up to this point her attitude leaves nothing to be desired, its practical effect is completely nullified by her insistence that the submission shall cover but a part of the controversy—that, as a condition of arbitrating her right to a part of the disputed territory, the remainder shall be turned over to her. If it were possible to point to a boundary which both parties have ever agreed or assumed to be such, either expressly or tacitly, the demand that territory conceded by such line to British Guiana should be held not to be in dispute might rest upon a reasonable basis. But there is no such line. The territory which Great Britain insists shall be conceded to her as a condition of arbitrating her claim to other territory, has never been admitted to belong to her. It has always and consistently been claimed by Venezuela. Upon what principle, except her feebleness as a nation, is she to be denied the right of having the claim heard and passed upon by an impartial tribunal? No reason or shadow of reason appears in all the voluminous literature of the subject. "It is to be so because I will it to be so" seems to be the only justification Great Britain offers.

PLEA OF LONG POSSESSION.

It is, indeed, intimated that the British claim to this particular territory rests upon an occupation which, whether acquiesced in or not, has ripened into a perfect title by long continuance. But what prescription affecting territorial rights can be said to exist as between sovereign states? Or, if there is any, what is the legitimate consequence? It is not that all arbitration should be denied, but only that the submission should embrace an additional topic, namely, the validity of the asserted prescriptive title, either in point of law or in point of fact. No different result follows from the contention that as a matter of principle Great Britain cannot be asked to submit and ought not to submit to arbitration her political sovereign rights over territory. This contention, as applied to the whole or a vital part of the possessions of a sovereign state need not be controverted. To hold otherwise might be equivalent to holding that a sovereign state was bound to arbitrate its very existence. But Great Britain has herself shown in various instances that the principle has no pertinency when either the interests or the territorial area involved are not of controlling magnitude, and her loss of them as the result of an arbitration cannot appreciably affect her honor or her power. Thus, she has arbitrated the extent of her colonial possessions, twice with the United States, twice with Portugal, and once with Germany and perhaps in other instances.

A PRECEDENT.

The Northwestern water boundary arbitration of 1872, between her and this country, is an example in point and well illustrates both the effect to be given to long-continued used and enjoyment and the fact that a truly great power sacrifices neither prestige nor dignity by reconsidering the most emphatic rejection of a proposition when satisfied of the obvious and intrinsic justice of the case. By the award of the Emperor of Germany, the arbitrator in that case, the United States acquired San Juan and a number of smaller islands near the coast of Vancouver as a consequence of the decision that the term "the channel which separates the continent from Vancouver's island," as used in the treaty of Washington of 1846, means the Haro channel and not the Rosario channel. Yet a leading contention of Great Britain before the arbitration was that equity required a judgment in her favor because a decision in favor of the United States would deprive British subjects of rights of navigation of which they had had the habitual enjoyment from the time when the Rosario strait was first explored and surveyed in 1798. So, though by virtue of the award the United State acquired San Juan and the other islands of the group to which it belongs, the British foreign secretary had, in 1859, instructed the British minister at Washington as follows:

Her majesty's government must, therefore, under any circumstances, maintain the right of the British crown to the island of San Juan. The interests at stake in connection with the retention of that island are too important to admit of compromise, and your lordship will consequently bear in mind that, whatever arrangement as to the boundary line is finally arrived at, no settlement of the question will be accepted by her majesty's government which does not provide for the island of San Juan being reserved to the British crown.

BRITAIN'S IPSE DIXIT.

Thus, as already intimated, the British demand that her right to a portion of the disputed territory shall be acknowledged before she will consent to an arbitration as to the rest, seems to stand upon nothing but her own ipse dixit. She says to Venezuela, in substance: "You can get none of the debatable land by force, because you are not strong enough; you can get none by treaty, because I will not agree; and you can take your chance of getting a portion by arbitration, only if you first agree to abandon to me such other portion as I may designate."

It is not perceived how such an attitude can be defended, nor how it is reconcilable with that love of justice and fair play so eminently characteristic of the English race. It, in effect, deprives Venezuela of her free agency and puts her under virtual duress. Territory acquired by reason of it will be as much wrested from her by the strong hand as if occupied by British troops or covered by British fleets.

It seems, therefore, quite impossible that this position of Great Britain should be assented to by the United States, or that, if such position be adhered to with the result of enlarging the bounds of British Guiana, it should not be regarded as amounting, in substance, to an invasion and conquest of Venezuelan territory.

In these circumstances, the duty of the president appears to him unmistakable and imperative. Great Britain's assertion of title to the disputed territory, combined with her refusal to have that title investigated, being a substantial appropriation of the territory to her own use, not to protest and give warning that the transaction will be regarded as injurious to the interests of the people of the United States as well as oppressive in itself would be to ignore an established policy with which the honor and welfare of this country are closely identified.

While the measures necessary or proper for the vindication of that policy are to be determined by another branch of the government, it is clearly for the executive to have nothing undone which may tend to render such determination unnecessary.

AN ANSWER DEMANDED.

You are instructed, therefore, to present the foregoing views to Lord Salisbury by reading to him this communication (leaving with him a copy should he so desire), and to reinforce them by such pertinent considerations as will doubtless occur to you. They call for a definite decision upon the point whether Great Britain will consent or will decline to submit the Venezuelan boundary question in its entirety to impartial arbitration. It is the earnest hope of the president that the conclusion will be on the side of arbitration, and that Great Britain will add one more to the conspicuous precedents she has already furnished in favor of that wise and just mode of adjusting international disputes.

If he is to be disappointed in that hope, however—a result not to be antici-

pated and in his judgment calculated to greatly embarrass the future relations between this country and Great Britain —it is his wish to be made acquainted with the fact at such early date as will enable him to lay the whole subject before Congress in his next annual message.

I am, sir, your obedient servant,
RICHARD OLNEY.

HINTS FROM MR. ADEE.

For Mr. Bayard's instruction Acting Secretary Adee wrote as follows:
(No. 806.)
Department of State,
Washington, July 24, 1895.
His Excellency, Thomas F. Bayard, Etc.,
Etc., Etc., London:

Sir—In Mr. Olney's instructions No. 804, of the 20th instant, in relation to the Anglo-Venezuelan boundary dispute, you will note a reference to the sudden increase of the area claimed for British Guiana, amounting to 33,000 square miles, between 1884 and 1886. This statement is made on the authority of the British publication entitled the Statesman's Year Book. I add for your better information that the same statement is found in the British Colonial Office List, a government publication. In the issue for 1885 the following passage occurred, on page 24, under the head of British Guiana:

It is impossible to specify the exact area of the colony, as its precise boundaries between Venezuela and Brazil respectively are undertermined, but it has been computed to be 76,000 square miles.

In the issue of the same List for 1886 the same statement occurs on page 33, with the change of area to "about 109,000 square miles."

The official maps in the two volumes mentioned are identical, so that the increase of 33,000 square miles claimed for British Guiana is not thereby explained, but later Colonial Office List maps show a varying sweep of the boundary westward into what previously figured as Venezuelan territory, while no change is noted on the Brazilian frontier. I am, sir, your obedient servant,
ALVEY A. ADEE, Acting Secretary.

SALISBURY'S FIRST NOTE.

States the Grounds of Great Britain's Refusal to Arbitrate.

Foreign Office, Nov. 26, 1895.

Sir—On the 7th of August I transmitted to Lord Gough a copy of the dispatch from Mr. Olney which Mr. Bayard had left with me that day, and of which he had read portions to me. I informed him at the time that it could not be answered until it had been carefully considered by the law officers of the crown. I have, therefore, deferred replying to it till after the recess.

I will not now deal with those portions of it which are concerned exclusively with the controversy that has for some time past existed between the republic of Venezuela and her majesty's government in regard to the boundary which separates their dominions. I take a very different view from Mr. Olney of various matters upon which he touches in that part of the dispatch, but I will defer for the present all observations upon it, as it concerns matters which are not in themselves of first-rate importance, and do not directly concern the relations between Great Britain and the United States.

The latter part, however, of the dispatch, turning from the question of the frontiers of Venezuela, proceeds to deal with the principles of a far wider character, and to advance doctrines of international law which are of considerable interest to all the nations whose dominions include any portion of the Western hemisphere. The contention set forth by Mr. Olney in this part of his dispatch are represented by him as being an application of the political maxims which are well known in American discussion under the name of the Monroe doctrine.

NOT MONROE'S DOCTRINE.

As far as I am aware, this doctrine has never been before advanced on behalf of the United States in any written communication addressed to the government of another nation, but it has been generally adopted and assumed as true by many eminent writers and politicians in the United States. It is said to have largely influenced the government of that country in the conduct of its foreign affairs, though Mr. Clayton, who was secretary of state under President Taylor, expressly stated that that administration had in no way adopted it. But during the period that has elapsed since the message of President Monroe was delivered, in 1823, the doctrine has undergone a very notable development, and the aspect which it now presents in the hands of Mr. Olney differs widely from its character when it first issued from the pen of its author. The two propositions which in effect President Monroe laid down were: (1) that America was no longer to be looked upon as a field for European colonization, and (2) that Europe must not attempt to extend its political system to America, or to control the political conditions of any of the American communities who had recently declared their independence.

The dangers against which President Monroe thought it right to guard were not as imaginary as they would seem at the present day. The formation of the Holy Alliance, the Congresses of Laybach and Verona, the invasion of Spain by France for the purpose of forcing upon the Spanish people a form of government which seemed likely to disappear unless it was sustained by external aid, were incidents fresh in the mind of President Monroe when he penned his celebrated message. The system of which he spoke, and of which he so resolutely deprecated the application to the American continent, was the system then adopted by certain powerful states upon the continent of Europe, of combining to prevent by force of arms the adoption in other countries of political institutions which they disliked, and to uphold by external pressure those which they approved.

Various portions of South America had recently declared their independence, and that independence had not been recognized by the governments of Spain and Portugal, to which, with small exceptions, the whole of Central and South America were nominally subject. It was not an imaginary danger that he foresaw, if he feared that the same spirit which had dictated the French expedition into Spain might inspire the more

owerful governments of Europe with
he idea of imposing, by the force of
rms, upon the South American communities the form of government and the
olitical connection which they had
hrown off. In declaring that the United
States would resist any such enterprise
f it were contemplated, President Mon-
oe adopted a policy which received the
ntire sympathy of the English government of that day.

COLONIZING NOT INTENDED.

The dangers which were apprehended
y President Monroe have no relation
o the state of things in which we live
t the present day. There is no dan-
er of any Holy Alliance imposing its
ystem upon any portion of the Ameri-
n continent, and there is no danger
f any European state treating any part
f the American continent as a fit object
r European colonization.
It is intelligible that Mr. Olney should
voke, in defense of the views on which
e is now insisting, an authority which
jjoys so high a popularity with his own
llow-countrymen. But the circum-
ances with which President Monroe
as dealing and those to which the pres-
nt American government is addressing
self, have very few features in common.
reat Britain is imposing no "system"
pon Venezuela, and is not concerning
erself in any way with the nature of the
olitical institutions under which the
enezuelans may prefer to live. But the
ritish empire and the republic of Vene-
ela are neighbors, and they have dif-
red for some time past, and continue to
ffer, as to the line by which their
ominions are separated.
It is a controversy with which the
nited States have no apparent prac-
al concern. It is difficult, indeed, to
e how it can materially affect any state
community outside those primarily
terested, except perhaps other parts of
r majesty's dominions, such as Trini-
d. The disputed frontier of Vene-
ela has nothing to do with any of the
estions dealt with by President Mon-
e. It is not a question of the coloniza-
on by any European power of any por-
on of America. It is not a question of
e imposition upon the communities of
uth America of any system of govern-
ent devised in Europe. It is simply
e determination of the frontier of a
ritish possession which belonged to
e throne of England long before the
public of Venezuela came into exist-
ce.

But even if the interests of Venezuela were so far linked to those of the
United States as to give to the latter a
locus standi in this controversy, their
government apparently has not formed,
and certainly does not express, any
opinion upon the actual merits of the dispute. The government of the United
States does not say that Great Britain
or that Venezuela is in the right in the
matters that are in issue. But it lays
down that the doctrine of President
Monroe, when he opposed the imposition
of European systems or the renewal of
European colonization confers upon
them the right of demanding that when
a European power has a frontier difference with a South American community the European power shall consent to refer that controversy to arbitration, and Mr. Olney states that unless
her majesty's government accede to this
demand it will "greatly embarrass the
future relations between Great Britain and the United States."

OLNEY'S POSITION NOT TENABLE.

Whatever may be the authority of the
doctrine laid down by President Monroe, there is nothing in his language to
show that he ever thought of claiming
this novel prerogative for the United
States. It is admitted that he did not
seek to assert a protectorate over Mexico or the states of Central and South
America. Such a claim would have im-
posed upon the United States the duty
of answering for the conduct of these
states, and consequently the responsibility of controlling it. His sagacious
foresight would have led him energetic-
ally to deprecate the addition of so serious a burden to those which the rulers
of the United States have to bear. It
follows of necessity that if the government of the United States will not control the conduct of these communities,
neither can it undertake to protect them
from the consequences attaching to any
misconduct of which they may be guilty
towards other nations.
If they violate in any way the rights
of another state or of its subjects, it is
not alleged that the Monroe doctrine will
assure them the assistance of the United
States in escaping from any reparation
which they may be bound by international law to give. Mr. Olney expressly disclaims such an inference from
the principles he lays down. But the
claim which he founds upon them is
that, if any independent American state
advances a demand for territory of

which its neighbor claims to be the owner, and that neighbor is a colony of a European state, the United States have a right to insist that the European state shall submit the demand and its own impugned rights, to arbitration.

ARBITRATION POLICY OPPOSED.

I will not now enter into a discussion of the merits of this method of terminating international differences. It has proved itself valuable in many cases, but it is not free from defects which often operate as a serious drawback on its value. It is not always easy to find an arbitrator who is competent, and who at the same time is wholly free from bias, and the task of insuring compliance with the award when it is made is not exempt from difficulty. It is a mode of settlement of which the value varies much according to the nature of the controversy to which it is applied and the character of the litigants who appeal to it. Whether, in any particular case, it is a suitable method of procedure, is generally a delicate and difficult question. The only parties who are competent to decide that question are the two parties whose rival contentions are in issue. The claim of a third nation, which is unaffected by the controversy, to impose this particular procedure on either of the two others cannot be reasonably justified, and has no foundation in the law of nations.

In the remarks which I have made I have argued on the theory that the Monroe doctrine in itself is sound. I must not, however, be understood 'as expressing an acceptance of it on the part of her majesty's government. It must always be mentioned with respect, on account of the distinguished statesmen to whom it is due and the great nations who have generally adopted it. But international law is founded on the general consent of nations, and no statesman, however eminent, and no nation, however powerful, are competent to insert into the code of international law a novel principle which was never recognized before, and which has not since been recognized by the government of any other country.

The United States has a right, like any other nation, to interpose in any controversy by which their own interests are affected, and they are the judge whether those interests are touched and in what measure they should be sustained. But their rights are in no way strengthened or extended by the fact that the controversy affects some territory which is called American. Mr. Olney quotes the case of the recent Chilian war, in which the United States declined to join with France and England in an effort to bring hostilities to a close on account of the Monroe doctrine. The United States were entirely in their right in declining to join in an attempt at pacification if they thought fit, but Mr Olney's principle that "American questions are for American decision," even if it received any countenance from the language of President Monroe (which it does not), cannot be sustained by any reasoning drawn from the law of nations.

UNITED STATES NOT CONCERNED

The government of the United States is not entitled to affirm as a universal proposition, with reference to a number of independent states for whose conduct it assumes no responsibility, that its interests are necessarily concerned in whatever may befall those states simply because they are situated in the western hemisphere. It may well be that the interests of the United States are affected by something that happens to Chili or Peru and that the circumstances may give them the right of interference; but such a contingency may equally happen in the case of China or Japan, and the right of interference is not more extensive or more assured in the one case than in the other.

Though the language of President Monroe is directed to the attainment of objects which most Englishmen would agree to be salutary, it is impossible to admit that they have been inscribed by any adequate authority in the code of international law, and the danger which such admission would involve is sufficiently exhibited both by the strange development which the doctrine has received at Mr. Olney's hands and the arguments by which it is supported in the dispatch under reply. In defense of ' he says: "That distance and 3,000 miles of intervening ocean make any permanent political union between a European and an American state unnatural and inexpedient will hardly be denied. But physical and geographical considerations are the least of the objections to such union. Europe has a set of primary interests which are peculiar to herself America is not interested in them, and ought not to be vexed or complicated with them." And again: "Thus far in our history we have been spared the hum dens and evils of immense standing armies and all the other accessories of huge warlike establishments, and the exemption has highly contributed to our national greatness and wealth, as well as to the happiness of every citizen. But with the powers of Europe permanently encamped on American soil the ideal conditions we have thus far enjoyed cannot be expected to continue."

UNION IS EXPEDIENT.

The necessary meaning of these words is that the union between Great Britain and Canada, between Great Britain and Jamaica and Trinidad, between Great Britain and British Honduras or British Guiana, is "inexpedient and unnatural." President Monroe disclaims any such inference from his doctrine, but in this as in other respects Mr. Olney develops it. He lays down that the inexpedient and unnatural character of the union between a European and an American state is so obvious that it "will hardly be denied."

Her majesty's government are prepared emphatically to deny it on behalf of both the British and American people who are subject to the crown. They maintain that the union between Great Britain and her territories in the western hemisphere is both natural and expedient. They fully concur with the view which President Monroe apparently entertained, that any disturbance of the existing territorial distribution in that hemisphere by any fresh acqui-

sitions on the part of any European state would be a highly inexpedient change. But they are not prepared to admit that the recognition of that expediency is clothed with the sanction which belongs to a doctrine of international law. They are not prepared to admit that the interests of the United States are necessarily concerned in every frontier dispute which may arise between any two of the states who possess dominion in the western hemisphere, and still less can they accept the doctrine that the United States are entitled to claim that the process of arbitration shall be applied to any demand for the surrender of territory which one of those states may make against another.

I have commented in the above remarks only upon the general aspect of Mr. Olney's doctrine, apart from the special considerations which attach to the controversy between the United Kingdom and Venezuela in its present phase. This controversy has undoubtedly been made more difficult by the inconsiderate action of the Venezuelan government in breaking off relations with her majesty's government, and its settlement has been correspondingly delayed; but her majesty's government have not surrendered the hope that it will be adjusted by a reasonable arrangement at an early date.

I request that you will read the subject of the above dispatch to Mr. Olney and leave him a copy if he desires it.
SALISBURY.

SALISBURY'S SECOND LETTER.

Says Olney's Narration of What Passed is Based on Ex Parte Statements.

"Foreign Office, Nov. 26, 1895.
Sir: In my preceding dispatch of to-day's date I have replied only to the latter portion of Mr. Olney's despatch of July 20 last, which treats of the application of the Monroe doctrine to the question of the boundary dispute between Venezuela and the colony of British Guiana. But it seems desirable, in order to remove some evident misapprehensions as to the main features of the question, that the statement of it contained

in the earlier portion of Mr. Olney's despatch should not be left without reply. Such a course will be the more convenient, because, in consequence of the suspension of diplomatic relations, I shall not have the opportunity of setting right misconceptions of this kind in the ordinary way in a despatch addressed to the Venezuelan government itself.

Her majesty's government, while it has never avoided or declined argument on the subject with the government of

Venezuela, has always held that the question was one which had no direct bearing on the material interests of any other country, and has consequently refrained hitherto from presenting any detailed statement of its case either to 'the United States or to other foreign governments. It is perhaps a natural consequence of this circumstance that Mr. Olney's narration of what has passed bears the impress of being mainly, if not entirely, founded on ex parte statements emanating from Venezuela, and gives, in the opinion of her majesty's government, an erroneous view of many material facts.

Mr. Olney commences his observations by remarking that 'the dispute is of ancient date, and began at least as early as the time when Great Britain acquired by the treaty with the Netherlands in 1814 the establishments of Demerara, Essequibo and Berbice. From that time to the present the dividing line between these establishments, now called British Guiana and Venezuela, has never ceased to be a subject of contention.'

OLNEY WRONG IN FACTS.

This statement is founded on misconception. The dispute on the subject of the frontier did not, in fact, commence till after the year 1840. The title of Great Britain to the territory in question is derived, in the first place, from conquest and military occupation of the Dutch settlements in 1796. Both on this occasion and at the time of a previous occupation of these settlements in 1781 the British authorities marked the western boundary of their possessions as beginning some distance up the Orinoco beyond Point Barima, in accordance with the limits claimed and actually held by the Dutch, and this has always since remained the frontier claimed by Great Britain.

The definite cession of the Dutch settlements to England was, as Mr. Olney states, placed on record by the treaty of 1814, and although the Spanish government were parties to the negotiations which led to that treaty, they did not at any stage of them raise objection to the frontiers claimed by Great Britain. though these were perfectly well known to them. At that time the government of Venezuela had not been recognized even by the United States, though the province was already ·in revolt against the Spanish government, and had declared its independence. No question of fron-

tier was raised with Great Britain either by it or by the government of the United States of Colombia, in which it became merged in 1819. That government, indeed, on repeated occasions, acknowledged its indebtedness to Great Britain for her friendly attitude. When in 1830 the republic of Venezuela assumed a separate existence its government was equally warm in its expressions of gratitude and friendship, and there was not at the time any indication of an intention to raise such claims as have been urged by it during the latter portion of this century.

VENEZUELA'S DECLARATIONS INVALID.

It is true, as stated by Mr. Olney, that in the Venezuelan constitution of 1830, article 5 lays down that 'the territory of Venezuela comprises all that which previously to the political changes of 1810 was denominated the Captaincy-General of Venezuela.' Similar declarations had been made in the fundamental laws promulgated in 1819 and 1821.

I need not point out that a declaration of this kind made by a newly self-constituted state can have no valid force as against international arrangements previously concluded by the nation from which it had separated itself.

But the present difficulty would never have arisen if the government of Venezuela had been content to claim only those territories which could be proved or even reasonably asserted to have been practically in the possession and under the effective jurisdiction of the Captaincy-General of Venezuela.

There is no authoritative statement by the Spanish government of those territories, for a decree which the Venezuelan government alleges to have been issued by the king of Spain in 1768, describing the province Guiana as bordered on the south by the Amazon and on the east by the Atlantic, certainly cannot be regarded as such. It absolutely ignores the Dutch settlements, which not only existed in fact, but had been formally recognized by the treaty of Munster of 1648, and it would, if now considered valid, transfer to Venezuela the whole of the British, Dutch and French Guianas, and an enormous tract of territory belonging to Brazil.

But of the territory claimed and actually occupied by the Dutch, which were those acquired from them by Great Britain, there exist the most authentic declarations. In 1759, and again in 1769, the states general of Holland addressed formal remonstrances to the court of Madrid against the incursions of the Spaniards into their posts and settlements in the basin of the Cuyuni. In those remonstrances they distinctly claimed all the branches of the Essequibo river, and especially the Cuyuni river, as lying within Dutch territory. They demanded immediate reparation for the proceedings of Spaniards and reinstatement of the posts said to have been injured by them, and suggested that a proper delineation between the colony of Essequibo and the Rio Orinoco should be laid down by authority.

To this claim the Spanish government never attempted to make any reply. But it is evident from the archives which are preserved in Spain and to which, by the courtesy of the Spanish government, reference has been made, that the council of state did not consider that they had the means of rebutting it, and that neither they nor the governor of Cumana were prepared seriously to maintain the claims which were suggested in reports from his subordinate officer, the commandant at Guiana. These reports were characterized by the Spanish ministers as insufficient and unsatisfactory as professing to show the province of Guiana under too favorable a light, and finally by the council of state as appearing from other information to be very improbable.

They form, however, with a map which accompanied them, the evidence on which the Venezuelan government appears most to rely, though it may be observed among other documents which have from time to time been produced or referred to by them in the course of the discussions is a bull of Pope Alexander VI. In 1493, which, if it is to be considered as having any present validity, would take from the government of the United States all titles to jurisdiction on the continent of North America. The fundamental principle underlying the argument is, in fact, that inasmuch as Spain was originally entitled of right to the whole of the American continent, any territory on that continent which she cannot be shown to have acknowledged in positive and specific terms to have passed to another power can only have been acquired by wrongful usurpation, and if situated to the north of the Amazon and west of the Atlantic, must necessarily belong to Venezuela as her self constituted inheritor in those regions.

ASKS OLNEY WHAT HE WOULD DO.

It may reasonably be asked whether Mr. Olney would consent to refer to the arbitration of another power pretensions received by the government of Mexico on such a foundation to large tracts of territory which had long been comprised in the federation.

The circumstances connected with the marking of what is called the 'Schomburgk' line are as follows:

In 1831 a grant was made by the British government for the exploration of the interior of the British colony, and Mr. (afterwards Sir) Schomburgk, who was employed in this service, on his return to the capital of the colony, in July, 1839, called the attention of the government to the necessity for an early demarcation of its boundaries. He was in consequence appointed in November, 1840, special commissioner for provisionally surveying and delimiting the boundaries of British Guiana, and notice of the appointment was given to the governments concerned, including that of Venezuela. The intention of her majesty's government at that time was, when the work of the commissioner had been completed, to communicate to the other governments its views as to the true boundary of the British colony, and then to settle any details to which those governments might take objection.

It is important to notice that Sir R. Schomburgk did not discover or invent any new boundaries. He took particular care to fortify himself with the history of the case. He had, further, from actual exploration and information obtained from the Indians, and from the evidence of local remains, as at Barima, and local traditions, as on the Cuyuni, fixed the limits of the Dutch possessions, and the zone from which all trace of Spanish influence was absent. On such data he bases his reports. At the very outset of his mission he surveyed Point Barima, where the remains of a Dutch fort still existed, and placed there and at the mouth of Amacura two boundary posts. At the urgent entreaty of the Venezuelan government these two posts were afterwards removed, as stated by Mr. Olney, but this concession was made on the distinct understanding that Great Britain did not thereby in any way abandon its claim to that position.

In submitting the maps of his survey on which he indicated the line which he would propose to her majesty's government for adoption, Sir R. Schomburgk called attention to the fact that her majesty's government might justly claim the whole basin of the Cuquni and Yuruari, on the ground that the natural boundary of the colony included any territory through which flows rivers which fall into the Essequibo. "Upon this principle," he wrote, "the boundary line would run from the sources of the Carumani towards the courses of the Cuyuni proper, and thence towards its far more northern tributaries, the rivers Iruary (Yutauari) and Iruangkiruang (Yuruan), and thus approach the very heart of Venezuelan Guiana." But on grounds of complaisance towards Venezuela he proposed that Great Britain should consent to surrender its claim to a more extended frontier inland in return for the formal recognition of her right to Point Barima. It was on this principle that he drew the boundary line which has since been called by his name.

THE SCHOMBURGK LINE.

Undoubtedly, therefore, Mr. Olney is right when he states that it seems impossible to treat the Schomburgk line, being the boundary claimed by Great Britain, as matter of right or as anything but a line originating in considerations of convenience and expediency. The Schomburgk line was in fact a great reduction of the boundary claimed by Great Britain as matter of right, and its proposal originated in a desire to come to a speedy and friendly arrangement with a weaker power with whom Great Britain was at the time, and desired to remain, in cordial relations.

The following are the main facts of the discussions that ensued with the Venezuela government. While Mr. Schomburgk was engaged on his survey the Venezuelan minister in London had urged her majesty's government to enter into a treaty of limits, but received the answer that if it should be necessary to enter into such a treaty, a survey was at any rate the necessary preliminary.

As soon as her majesty's government were in possession of Mr. Schomburgk's report, the Venezuelan minister was informed that they were in a position to commence negotiations, and in January, 1844, Mr. Fortique commenced by stating the claim of his government. This claim, starting from such obsolete grounds as the original discovery by Spain of the American continent, and mainly supported by quotations of a more or less vague character from the writings of travelers and geography, but adducing no substantial evidence of actual conquest or occupation of the territory claimed, demanded the Essequibo itself as the boundary of Venezuela.

A reply was returned by Lord Aberdeen, then secretary of state for foreign affairs, pointing out that it would be impossible to arrive at any agreement if both sides brought forward pretensions of so extreme a character, but stating that the British government would not imitate Mr. Fortique in putting forward a claim which it could not be intended seriously to maintain. Lord Aberdeen then proceeded to announce the concessions which, out of friendly regard to

Venezuela, her majesty's government were prepared to make, and proposed a line starting from the mouth of the Moroco to the junction of the river Barama with the Waini, thence up the Barama to the point at which that stream approached nearest to the Acarabisi, and thence following Sir R. Schomburgk's line from the source of the Acarabisi onward.

WHAT ENGLAND OFFERED.

A condition was attached to the proffered cession, viz., that the Venezuelan government should enter into an engagement that no portion of the territory proposed to be ceded should be alienated at any time to a foreign power and that the Indian tribes residing in it should be protected from oppression. No answer to the note was ever received from the Venezuelan government, and in 1850 her majesty's government informed her majesty's charge d'affairs at Caracas that as the proposal had remained for more than six years unaccepted it must be considered as having lapsed, and authorized him to make a communication to the Venezuelan government to that effect.

A report having at the time become current in Venezuela that Great Britain intended to seize Venezuelan Guiana, the British government distinctly disclaimed such an intention, but inasmuch as the government of Venezuela subsequently permitted projects to be set on foot for the occupation of Point Barima and certain other positions in dispute, the British charge d'affairs was instructed in June, 1850, to call the serious attention of the president and government of Venezuela to the question and to declare to them, "that whilst on the one hand, Great Britain had no intention to occupy or encroach on the disputed territory, she would not on the other hand view with indifference aggressions on that territory by Venezuela."

The Venezuelan government replied in December of the same year that Venezuela had no intention of occupying or encroaching upon any part of the territory the dominion of which was in dispute, and that orders would be issued to the authorities in Guiana to abstain from taking any steps contrary to this engagement. This constitutes what has been termed the agreement of 1850, to which the government of Venezuela have frequently appealed, but which the

Venezuelans have repeatedly violated in succeeding years. Their first acts of this nature consisted in the assumption of positions to the east of their previous settlements and the founding in 1858 of the town of Nueva Providencia on the right bank of the Yuruari, all previous settlements being on the left bank. The British government, however, considering that these settlements were so near positions which they had not wished to claim, considering also the difficulty of controlling the bounds of mining populations, overlooked this breach of the agreement.

The governor of the colony was, in 1857, sent to Caracas to negotiate for a settlement of the boundary, but he found the Venezuelan state in so disturbed a condition that it was impossible to commence negotiations, and eventually he came away without having effected anything. For the next nineteen years, as stated by Mr. Olney, the civil commotions in Venezuela prevented any resumption of negotiations. In 1876 it was reported that the Venezuelan government had for the second time broken the agreement of 1850 by granting licenses to trade and cut wood in Barima and eastward.

Later in the same year that government once more made an overture for the settlement of the boundary. Various delays interposed before negotiations actually commenced, and it was not till 1879 that Senor Rojaz began them with a renewal of the claim to the Essequibo as the eastern boundary of Venezuelan Guiana. At the same time he stated that his government wished to obtain by means of a treaty a definitive settlement of the question and was disposed to proceed to the demarcation of the divisional line between the two Guianas in a spirit of conciliation and true friendship towards her majesty's government.

In reply to this communication a note was addressed to Senor Rojaz on January 10, 1880, reminding him that the boundary which her majesty's government claimed, as a matter of strict right on grounds of conquest and concessions by treaty, commenced at a point at the mouth of the Orinoco, westward of Point Barima, that it proceeded thence in a southerly direction to the Imataca mountains, the line of which it followed to the northwest, passing from thence by the highland of Santa Maria, just south of the town of Upata, until it struck a range of hills on the eastern bank of the Caroni river, followed thence southward until it struck the great backbone of the Cuiana district, the Barima mountains of British Guiana and thence southward to the Pacaraima mountains.

On the other hand, the claim which had been put forward on behalf of Venezuela by General Guzman Blanco in his message to the national congress of February 20, 1877, would involve the surrender of a province now inhabited by 40,000 British subjects, and which had been in the uninterrupted possession of Holland and of Great Britain successively for two centuries. The difference between these two claims being so great, was pointed out to Senor Rojaz that, in order to arrive at a satisfactory arrangement, each party must be prepared to make very considerable concessions to the other, and he was assured that, although the claim

of Venezuela to the Essequibo river boundary could not, under any circumstances, be entertained, yet that her majesty's government were anxious to meet the Venezuelan government in the spirit of conciliation, and would be willing, in the event of a renewal of negotiations for the general settlement of boundaries, to waive a portion of what they considered to be their strict rights, if Venezuela were really disposed to make corresponding concessions on her part.

VENEZUELA WAS OBDURATE.

The Venezuelan minister replied in February, 1881, by proposing a line which commenced on the coast a mile to the north of the Moroco river, and followed by certain parallels and meridians inland, bearing a general resemblance to the proposal made by Lord Aberdeen in 1844.

Senor Rojaz's proposal was referred to the lieutenant governor and attorney general of British Guiana, who were then in England, and they presented an elaborate report, showing that in the thirty-five years which elapsed since Lord Aberdeen's proposed concession, natives and others had settled in the territory under the belief that they would enjoy the benefits of English rule, and that it was impossible to assent to any such concessions, as Senor Rojaz's line would involve. They, however, proposed an alternative line, which involved considerable reductions of that laid down by Sir R. Schomburgk. This boundary was proposed to the Venezuelan government by Lord Granville in September, 1881, but no answer was ever returned by that government to the proposal.

While, however, the Venezuelan minister constantly stated that the matter was under active consideration, it was found that in the same year a concession had been given by his government to General Pulgar, which included a large portion of the territory in dispute. This was the third breach by Venezuela of the agreement of 1850. Early in 1884 news arrived of a fourth breach by Venezuela of the agreement of 1850, through two different grants which covered the whole of the territory in dispute, and as this was followed by actual attempts to settle on the disputed territory the British government could no longer remain inactive.

WARNING GIVEN.

Warning was therefore given to the Venezuelan government and to the concessionaries, and a British magistrate was sent into the threatened district to assert the British rights. Meanwhile the negotiations for a settlement of the boundary had continued, but the only replies that could be obtained from Senor Guzman Blanco, the Venezuelan minister, were proposals for arbitration in different forms, all of which her majesty's government were compelled to decline as involving a submission to the arbitration of the claim advanced by Venezuela in 1844 to all territory up to the left bank of the Essequibo.

British subjects made a decision of some kind absolutely necessary, and as the

As the progress of settlement by Venezuelan government refused to come to any reasonable arrangement, her majesty's government decided not to repeat the offer of concessions which had not been reciprocated, but to assert her undoubted right to the territory within the Schomburgk line, while still consenting to hold open for further negotiation, and even for arbitration, the unsettled lands between that line and what they considered to be the rightful boundary as stated in the note to Senor Rojaz of January 10, 1880.

The execution of this design was deferred for a time, owing to the return of Senor Guzman Blanco to London, and the desire of Lord Rosebery, then secretary of state for foreign affairs, to settle all pending questions between the two governments.

Mr. Olney is mistaken in supposing that in 1886 a treaty was practically agreed upon containing a general arbitration clause under which the parties might have submitted the boundary dispute to the decision of a third power, or of several powers in amity with both. It is true that General Guzman Blanco proposed that the commercial treaty between the two countries should contain a clause of this nature, but it had reference to future disputes only. Her majesty's government have always insisted on a separate decision of the frontier question, and have considered its settlement to be a necessary preliminary to other arrangements.

LORD ROSEBERY'S PROPOSAL.

Lord Rosebery's proposal, made in July, 1886, was that the two governments should agree to consider the territory lying between the boundary lines respectively proposed in the eighth paragraph of Senor Rojaz's note of February 21, 1881, and in Lord Granville's note of September 15, 1881, as the territory in dispute between the two countries, and that a boundary line within the limits of this territory should be traced either by an arbitrator or by a joint commission on the basis of an equal division of this territory, due regard being had to natural boundaries. Senor Guzman Blanco replied, declining the proposal, and repeating that arbitration on the whole claim of Venezuela was the only method of solution which he would suggest.

This pretension is hardly less exorbitant than would be a refusal by Great Britain to agree to an arbitration on the boundary of British Columbia and Alaska, unless the United States would consent to bring into question one-half of the whole area of the latter territory. He shortly afterwards left England and as there seemed no hope of arriving at an agreement by further discussions, the Schomburgk line was proclaimed as the irreducible boundary of the colony in October, 1886.

It must be borne in mind that in taking this step her majesty's government did not assert anything approaching their extreme claim, but confined themselves within the limits of what had as early as 1840 been suggested as a concession out of friendly regard and compliance. When Senor Guzman Blanco having returned to Venezuela, announced his intention of erecting a light house at Point Barima, the British government expressed their readiness to permit this if he would enter into a formal written agreement that its erection would not be held to prejudice their claim to the site. In the meanwhile the Venezuelan government had sent commissioners into the territory to the east of the Schomburgk line, and upon their return two notes were addressed to the British minister at Caracas, dated respectively the 26th and 30th of January, 1887, demanding the evacuation of the whole territory held by Great Britain from the mouth of the Orinoco to the Pomeroon river, and adding that should this not be done by February 20, and should the evacuation not be accompanied by the acceptance of arbitration as the means of deciding the pending frontier question, diplomatic relations would be broken off.

THE DIPLOMATIC RUPTURE.

In pursuance of this decision the British representative at Caracas received his passports and relations were declared by the Venezuelan government to be suspended on February 21, 1887.

In December of that year, as a matter of precaution and in order that the claims of Great Britain beyond the Schomburgk line might not be considered to have been abandoned, a notice was issued by the governor of British Guiana formally reserving those claims No steps have, however, at any time been taken by the British authorities to exercise jurisdiction beyond the Schomburgk line, nor to interfere with the proceedings of the Venezuelans in the territory outside of it, although, pending a settlement of the dispute, Great Britain cannot recognize these proceedings as valid, or as conferring any legitimate title.

The question has remained in this position ever since. The basis on which her majesty's government were prepared to negotiate for its settlement were clearly indicated to the Venezuelan plenipotentiaries who were successively dispatched to London in 1890, 1891, and 1893 to negotiate for a renewal of diplomatic relations, but as on those occasions the only solutions which the Venezuelan government professed themselves ready to accept would still have involved the submission to arbitration of the Venezuelan claim to a large portion of the British colony, no progress has yet been made towards a settlement.

It will be seen from the preceding statement that the government of Great Britain have from the first held the same view as to the extent of the territory which they are entitled to claim as a matter of right. It comprised the coast line up to the river Amacure and the whole basin of the Essequibo river and its tributaries. A portion of that claim, however, they have always been willing to waive altogether; in regard to another portion they have been and continue to be perfectly ready to submit the question of their title to arbitration.

RIGHTS NOT OPEN TO QUESTION.

As regards the rest, that which lies within the so-called Schomburgk line, they do not consider that the rights of Great Britain are open to question. Even within that line they have, on various occasions, offered to Venezuela considerable concessions as a matter of friendship and conciliation, and for the purpose of securing an amicable settlement of the dispute.

If, as time has gone on, the concessions thus offered diminished in extent and have now been withdrawn, this has been the necessary consequence of the gradual spread over the country of British settlements, which her majesty's government cannot, in justice to the inhabitants, offer to surrender to foreign rule; and the justice of such withdrawal is amply borne out by the researches in the national archives of Holland and Spain, which have furnished further and more convincing evidence in support of the British claims.

The discrepancies in the frontiers assigned to the British colony in various maps published in England and erroneously assumed to be founded on official information are easily accounted for by the circumstances which I have mentioned. Her majesty's government cannot, of course, be responsible for such publications made without its authority. ity.

Although the negotiations in 1890, 1891 and 1893 did not lead to any result, her majesty's government have not abandoned the hope that they may be resumed with better success, and that when the internal politics of Venezuela are settled on a more durable basis than has lately appeared to be the case, her government may be enabled to adopt a more moderate and conciliatory course in regard to this question than that of their predecessors.

Her majesty's government are sincerely desirous of being on friendly relations with Venezuela, and certainly have no design to seize territory that forcibly belongs to her or forcibly to extend sovereignty over any portion of her population.

THE SUMMARY.

They have, on the contrary, repeatedly expressed their readiness to submit to arbitration the conflicting claims of Great Britain and Venezuela to large tracts of territory which from their auriferous nature are known to be of almost untold value. But they cannot consent to entertain, or to submit to the arbitration of another power or of foreign jurists, however eminent, claims based on the extravagant pretensions of Spanish officials in the last century, and involving the transfer of large numbers of British subjects, who have for many years enjoyed the settled rule of a British colony, to a nation of different race and language, whose political system is subject to frequent disturbance, and whose institutions, as yet, too often afford very inadequate protection to life and property.

No issue of this description has ever been involved in the questions which Great Britain and the United States have consented to submit to arbitration, and her majesty's government are convinced that in similar circumstances the government of the United States would be equally firm in declining to entertain proposals of such a nature.

Your excellency is authorized to state the substance of this dispatch to Mr. Olney and to leave him a copy of it if he should desire it. I am, etc.,

"SALISBURY."